GUNHAWKS WESTWARD

Along the far reaches of the Chisholm Trail, from Kansas to Texas, the frontier was wide open — and waiting like vultures were the crooked bankers, mortgage holders and land grabbers. Kent Michener was being pushed off his range. He needed a good man he could trust, a man who was quick with a gun. And when a stranger rode in with the mark of the gun-fighter all over him, Michener didn't think it was any of his business to ask questions about the man's past. He didn't know the half of it!

CLEM HANNAH

GUNHAWKS WESTWARD

Complete and Unabridged

LINFORD
Leicester

First hardcover edition published in Great Britain
in 2003 by Robert Hale Limited, London

Originally published in paperback as
Gunhawks Westward by Chuck Adams

First Linford Edition
published 2004
by arrangement with
Robert Hale Limited, London

British Library CIP Data

Hannah, Clem
    Gunhawks westward.—Large print ed.—
Linford western library
1. Western stories 2. Large type books
I. Title II. Adams, Chuck
823.9′14 [F]

ISBN 1–84395–476–1

Published by
F. A. Thorpe (Publishing)
Anstey, Leicestershire

Set by Words & Graphics Ltd.
Anstey, Leicestershire
Printed and bound in Great Britain by
T. J. International Ltd., Padstow, Cornwall

This book is printed on acid-free paper

1

Bullet Lash

The morning had been hot but now it was the height of noon and the heat beat down on the three men with a savage intensity. Here, in the valley, there was no breeze, no shade, and it was like riding directly into a scorching oven.

'Oh, my jiminy, it's hot,' said Denver, grimacing. His eyes were half-closed, breath falling in fitful gasps from his dry, cracked lips. Across his face the hot air fanned bluntly, merely ruffling the red hair showing beneath the wide-brimmed hat.

Kent Michener drew in a breath through his open mouth. 'We'll be at the creek in a little while. We'll rest up there and then head back if we don't find anythin'.'

'You expectin' to find Sam still around?' Carruthers spoke for the first time in an hour. He was a stocky, taciturn man, mainly keeping his thoughts to himself. 'I figure he just forked his bronc out durin' the night.'

'Maybe, but it ain't like any man to ride out without collectin' what wages are due to 'em.'

Carruthers shrugged his shoulders, sat hunched forward in the saddle, and said nothing more. Inwardly, he was quite certain that Sam Merritt had simply taken all he could and then lit out, maybe feeling that a whole skin was much preferable to losing his wages. Too many of the Lazy T crew had been bushwhacked during the past few months.

As they drew closer to the creek their horses quickened their pace from a lope to an almost eager gallop. The tremendous sunblast of the Texas high noon was an inverted furnace that sent down tremoring waves of heat on to the burnt ground, pressing and enveloping them, dredging up every last drop of moisture from their bodies.

Here, at the very southern edge of the Lazy T spread, the grassland had given way to an eroded stretch of rocky ground, with a copper-coloured soil that lay thinly on top of solid rock, enabling very little vegetation to grow. Only thin tufts of a wiry grass succeeded in surviving along this perimeter, but to the north, as they swung their mounts around the spread, there was a dense, dark green belt that formed a natural barrier between the desert and the range. It was composed mostly of thickets and mesquite, Spanish Sword and patches of *junco*, interspersed with prickly pear.

A swarm of vicious brown flies surged about them as they rode into the tangle of vegetation. Turning the sharp bend in the trail which led to the creek, Michener gave his mount its head, then reined up sharply. The fence that was strung out across the trail had been newly erected. The posts, driven firmly into the ground were of recently cut oak, and by the side of the trail he glimpsed the pile of shavings. There were four taut strands of shining wire that shone with a harsh glitter of reflected sunlight between the posts. Beyond them the rushing water of the creek bubbled over the stony bed, running fast between the eroded banks where the water had washed some of the thin topsoil away, exposing the bare rocks.

For a long moment Michener sat high in his saddle, staring in disbelief at the fence. His first thought was that some of the nesters had done this. They seemed to delight in fencing up the rangeland, claiming it was their property by Government decree, but as he let his gaze wander along the fence, arrow-straight for perhaps forty feet in both directions and then anglng back across the creek, he was forced to the conclusion that this was not the case. This was the work of somebody much bigger than any of the settlers in this part of the territory.

'Some of Klagge's work, boss?' muttered Carruthers grimly.

'It sure looks like it.' Michener's lips formed a grim line. 'He's been anglin' for this for a long time. He threatened he'd run every rancher off the range. First he started by bushwhackin' my men — and now this.'

'I'll come by with some of the boys tomorrow and take it down,' said Denver. 'Guess it must've been put up within the last two days.'

'If that's so, why didn't Sam ride in and tell us?' mused Michener. He sat forward in the saddle, while the two men stepped down, worked their riatas over two of the stout posts, then hitched the other ends to their saddles and backed their mounts away. The ropes tautened under the pull, taking up the slack. Then, with a rending screech, both posts came out of the ground, the wire bending and trailing on the ground, leaving a gap perhaps twenty feet wide in the fence.

Riding through, they swung down from the saddle at the edge of the stream, letting their horses blow. Carruthers squatted on his heels by the edge of the stream, built a smoke, letting his gaze wander over the small clearing on the far side of the stream. After a moment, he got to his feet, walked to the very edge of the water and stared across before calling to Michener.

'What is it?' asked the rancher. He was lighting a cigar, but held it and let the match burn down in his hand.

Carruthers pointed. 'Trail yonder, boss. Looks like a lot of men and horses.'

The other lit his cigar and drew deeply on it, letting the smoke out slowly through his open mouth. 'Now which way would they go from here?'

'You wouldn't think they'd head across the Lazy T range.'

'So they'd move their horses along the bank of the creek, then head for some distance through the water to hide their tracks.'

'That's the way I'd figure it.' Carruthers nodded.

Michener shrugged. 'Reckon you'd better get over there and take a look. Those tracks may still be fresh enough to give some clue to their identity.'

Carruthers whistled up his mount, swung up into the saddle, then gigged the horse across the shallow creek. On the far side he bent low in the saddle, peering closely at the ground. Presently, twenty feet or so from the creek, he came upon the remains of a fire that had been smothered out and, close to him, at the edge of the clearing, the tough, springy grass had been trampled out and broken off where the horses had been tethered.

Where the narrow trail left the clearing and twisted northward, his horse pricked up its ears and turned its head sharply. There came a low, neighing whinny from somewhere in the brush. Dropping from the saddle, his sixgun out, Carruthers went cautiously forward, the hammer of the Colt thumbed back. The horse was ground-reined near a tangled clump of mesquite, the emptiness of the saddle somehow enhanced by the bright silver trappings and gleaming stirrups that swung slowly to every movement the animal made.

It was undoubtedly Sam Merritt's horse. There was no mistaking it. Sam's mount was one of the best-dressed in the outfit, just as Sam always prided himself on being dandily dressed. Cautiously, Carruthers, stared about him. Just where was Merritt? He moved quietly, skirting the thick brush around the clearing, listening intently, every sense strained to the very limit, but the stillness was absolute.

Behind him the other two men came splashing across the creek, Michener leading. Carruthers pointed ahead as the men got down. Then he moved into the thick brush, scouting through the tangle. It was not much more than fifty yards from where he had found the horse that Carruthers came across Merritt's body. The cowpuncher was lying face down in a clump of Spanish Sword his back arched a little as if in the last spasm of death, his fingers clutching spasmodically at the narrow, sharp-edged leaves under him.

'Over this way,' Carruthers yelled harshly. 'I've found him!'

A crashing in the brush and then the others came up. Michener went down on one knee beside Merritt's body, gently turned him over, his features set in grim, hard lines. When he looked up again, his eyes were dark and empty. 'Shot in the chest from close range.'

'His gun is still in its holster,' Denver pointed out. 'Reckon it's a clear enough case of dry-gulchin'.'

'He must've come up on 'em when they was stringin' that fence along the creek,' Denver opined. 'If it was some of Klagge's men, they'd have posted look-outs along the trail in case of trouble.'

Michener did not answer, but straightened up and looked across the stretch of vegetation. 'Somebody is goin' to pay for this,' he gritted, squinting towards the trees. His face was without expression. 'Get his horse and set him on it. We'll take him back to the ranch and give him a decent burial.'

Between them the two men lifted Sam Merritt's body from the ground and laid it face down across the bay's saddle. Denver lashed it on with the saddle rope, tightened it securely.

With the bay picking its way carefully forward, its feet cut by the Spanish Sword in which it had been ground-reined, the going back to the ranch was slow, and it was close to five o'clock when the three men dipped over the final ridge, down to the sprawling houses of the Michener ranch.

'Take him into the barn and then come into the house,' Michener ordered. 'There's some things I want to talk over with you.'

Going into the house, Michener lit the lamp on the table near the window, then lowered himself in his high-backed chair, legs thrust out in front of him beneath the table. He could hear Stella humming to herself in the small kitchen and there was the appetising smell of stew cooking in the pot, but right now it had little effect on him. Since her mother had died two years before, Kent had lived for nothing but Stella and the ranch. When he died everything would belong to her and to her husband if she should marry. He had wanted her to stay out East at the finishing school to which he had sent her when she was thirteen, but six years later she had returned when Emma had been taken seriously ill, and she had stayed with him ever since, sometimes, as now, when things were rough, against his will. Trouble was, he thought with a faint smile, there was too much of his own fierce pride and self-will in her. Emma had been a small, dainty woman, little used to the ways of the frontier, but this was not so with Stella. She could ride a horse as well as any man, and he knew she was an excellent shot with a Winchester.

But with Klagge bearing down on him, life was too dangerous now for her to stay. Klagge was not a man to make idle threats and those he did make he could always back up with force.

Denver and Carruthers came into the room at the same moment that the kitchen door opened and Stella came in. 'I'll have dinner ready in — ' she began, then saw the expression on her father's face, and stopped, looking from one man to the other. When no one spoke, she went on, hesitantly: 'Something's wrong, isn't it?'

'Better go back and finish gettin' the dinner ready, Stella,' said Kent heavily. 'I've somethin' to talk over with the boys and — '

'Something you can't say with me here, is that it?' Her tone was taut and challenging. 'If it concerns the ranch, then surely it concerns me.'

A sort of grey bleakness settled over the older man. At length he nodded his head slowly. 'Yes,' he admitted, 'I guess it does, Stella. We found Sam Merritt out on the south perimeter. He'd been shot down from ambush.'

'Sam's dead?'

'Afraid so, Miss Stella,' put in Carruthers softly. 'We brought him back and we'll bury him tomorrow.'

'But why would anyone want to kill him?' The girl's brow was furrowed in perplexity. 'Sam never did any man the least bit of harm. He was a good rider.'

Kent Michener sat at the table, his strong, craggy features highlighted with shadow in the yellow glow of the lamp. 'There's a fence strung along the creek where we found Sam's body. We think he must've come on the men responsible and they shot him down in cold blood.'

'Austen Klagge.' It was more of a statement of fact than a question.

'There's no real proof.' Her father spread his hands wide in a futile gesture. 'Even if I was to go to Sheriff Tracer and lodge an official complaint, there's not much he can do. The only man who could possibly have identified them is lying dead in the barn right now.'

'But you're not going to let that fence stay there, on our land?'

'The boys will take it down tomorrow.' He lifted his head and looked directly at her, and now there was a new expression on his face which she had never seen before, one which was a little frightening because she did not understand it. 'Better see to your work in the kitchen, Stella.'

He waited until she had gone, then turned to the two hands. 'Sit down, boys. This is somethin' we've got to talk over right now. I think you can guess what I've got on my mind.'

It was Denver, the taciturn, who nodded. 'The rest of the boys aren't goin' to like it when they hear that Sam was shot down like that, without even a chance to draw his gun. From what I know of most of 'em, they won't want to stay around here to wait for the same thing to happen to them.'

'I know. That's what I've got on my mind. You can be damned certain that Klagge knows it too.'

Carruthers jerked his head up angrily. 'If he really pulls out all of the stops, you don't have a chance in hell of fightin' him. Those men he's hired are all professional killers, every last man. We're cowpunchers. That's our business. We can use our guns in a showdown, but we don't match up to them.'

Mitchener paused for a moment, then glanced across the table at Denver. 'That the way you feel as well, Bucko?'

The other shrugged. 'There's plenty of sense in what Ben says. You hired me to ride herd for you, mend fences, round up and brand the strays. I ain't no gunhawk.'

Michener scowled as if he did not understand or did not agree. Getting to his feet, he walked over to the window, stood there with his hands clasped tightly behind his back. His tone was bitter. 'This was little more than desert when I first came here. I built all of this, the ranch, the herd, everything. I made an empire out of the wilderness, and I don't intend to let a man like Austen Klagge run me out. If it comes to a showdown, then I'll remain here and fight him single-handed.' There was a savage intensity in his tone. 'I try to get along with everybody, but since Klagge moved into the valley he's done nothin' but try to run everybody out, to move in himself as lord of everythin'.'

'So what do you intend to do about it?' asked Carruthers shortly.

Michener smiled at him very slightly, lips drawn into a thin line of determination. 'I figure that the only way to deal with Klagge is to fight fire with fire. I aim to hire myself a few men handy with a gun; reckon there ought to be some hangin' around the saloons in Fresno City.'

'If Klagge ain't got 'em all on his

payroll,' put in Denver.

'I'll find somebody who ain't scared to stand up to the kind of men who ride with Klagge,' said Michener at length.

*   *   *

Laredo Ford saw the three men first because he was sitting facing the door of the saloon. Austen Klagge was on Ford's right and then, around the card table, were Fent Corday, the lawyer, Jose Rand and Tom Felder. Klagge dealt the cards around the table, looked up sharply at Ford's soft whisper, then slowly turned his head to look at the door. His lips stretched in a thinly derisive smile.

'I sort of figured he might show up some time,' he said softly, his voice soft so that it did not carry beyond the men gathered around him. 'Reckon he must've come across the fence.'

'What do you figure he'll do?' asked Corday cautiously. 'You don't think he's come for a showdown here in the saloon?'

'You scared there might be gunplay with you caught in the middle?' sneered the other.

'Well — no, but I'm no gunman and — '

'Then just sit tight and leave all of the talkin' — and the action — to us.' Klagge's narrow face grinned again, a little more viciously this time. His restless eyes watched as Michener and the two men with him walked over to the bar. His shadowed gaze eyed the Colts worn by all three men and, inwardly, he wondered just how far he would have to push Michener to make the big man go for his gun, so that the boys with him might shoot him down in self-defence. He knew that as far as men like Laredo and Jose were concerned, it would not be a matter of self-defence, that the three men stand-ing against the bar, talking now in low tones to Idaho Jones, the bartender, would be dead before any of them could get their guns half-drawn from their holsters. But in Fresno City, with Clem Duprey as Sheriff, things would have to appear legal on the surface.

Turning momentarily back to the game, he tossed a couple of chips into the pot in the middle of the table, said briefly: 'I call you, Corday.'

The lawyer faced his cards. 'Three queens,' he said softly, reached forward to rake the chips towards him, stopped as the rancher put out a hand and caught his wrist. 'Straight flush,' he said thinly.

Corday hesitated, then forced himself stiffly back into his chair. 'That beats me, I guess.'

Making a quick movement with his left hand, Klagge scooped the pool towards him and then, without turning his head, he called loudly: 'Hear you've been havin' a little trouble on your spread, Kent. Nothin' too bad, I hope.'

At the bar, Michener looked round slowly. For a moment there was a deep-seated anger stirring in him, threatening to blot out everything else. Then he forced evenness into his tone, knowing that the other was just trying to rile him. 'Wasn't nothin' me and the boys can't handle, Klagge.'

'Glad to hear it. Wouldn't like to think you were findin' things a little too much for you, especially now that the bank is startin' to call in some of the notes they have on the ranches because of the drought.'

Involuntarily, Michener looked at the other surprised, then his eyes half closed down. 'Haven't heard anythin' about that,' he said cautiously.

'Only heard it from Vickers myself this afternoon. Seems they got word from their head office to call in some of the notes now that the smaller ranches are goin' under.'

Michener remained silent. He had heard nothing official from the bank, but suddenly these words of Klagge's brought everything out into the open, made the veiled threat as definite as it could ever be without being spoken outright. Vickers, the banker in Fresno City, would do all that Klagge told him to do. Klagge was one of the largest, if not the largest, of the depositors in the bank and even the head office would know that if he took it into his head to withdraw all of his money, the consequences for the bank would be disastrous. It would have been Klagge's going to the bank and giving his orders which would have been the reason for this sudden change of attitude. Previously in any other years when there had been a particularly intense and prolonged drought, the demand notes had been waived whenever they had fallen due, extended to the time when the drought eased and things got better.

'Shouldn't be too hard on you, Michener,' Klagge went on, his tone almost a purr. 'From what I hear, you've got plenty of water in that creek runnin' along the southern edge of the Lazy T spread and you'll be able to see this drought through better than most. That is, unless the stories I've heard are

21

true and somebody is rustlin' your cattle and scarin' off your men.'

'Seems to be that you've been listenin' to some old maids' tales.' Michener pushed himself away from the bar and advanced towards the card table standing behind Jose Rand so that he could look across directly at Klagge. The anger was still seething away inside him, struggling to dominate both his thoughts and actions, but he kept it under rigid control with a tremendous effort of will, knowing that Klagge was just waiting for him to lose his head and try something rash. He forced himself to remember why he had ridden into town tonight — to try to sign up some men who would help him stand against this man who sat perfectly at his ease, grinning contemptuously at him.

Klagge opened his eyes wide in a look of feigned astonishment 'Then it ain't true?'

Michener shrugged. 'Some of the boys have been shot at from ambush, and one or two head of cattle have gone off, but this happens every year. Only thing that worries me right now is that fence you've strung up on my land.'

Klagge was still looking at Michener. The expression of sneering disdain vanished abruptly and his eyes narrowed into a look of anger. 'You sayin' I put up a fence on your spread, Michener?' he demanded.

'That's right,' Michener said quietly. 'We also found Sam Merritt where your boys had shot him down from cover.'

Klagge sat back in his chair and folded his arms elaborately over his chest. 'Now you've got proof of this, I suppose?'

'All the proof that I need, Klagge. I'm givin' you fair warnin' here and now. If I see you or any of your hired gunslingers on the Lazy T spread from today, I'll have them shot down.'

Laredo Ford, sitting low in his chair, had been fingering his chips absently. Now he said to nobody in particular, 'Sounds like a real tough one.' His glance slid sideways to Klagge. 'For my money, it's time he was taught a lesson.'

Michener turned sharply to face this new threat. He said thinly: 'What sort of lesson did you have in mind, Ford? A bullet in the back like you've dealt out to so many others because you're scared to meet 'em face to face with an even chance?'

Ford's clenched fist crashed down on the top of the table in front of him spilling the neat piles of chips and sending some scattering to the floor. Thrusting back his chair, he got heavily to his feet, eyes blazing savagely. His right hand dropped swiftly to his gunbutt, fingers clawing around it.

'Laredo!' Klagge's voice cut through the short silence like the lash of a whip. 'I'll handle this in my own way.'

'Maybe your way won't be good enough for this *hombre*,' Laredo said harshly. He still wanted to make a play for his gun. It showed in the fierce, hungry look in his eyes and the curved fingers still less than an inch above the gun.

'What's wrong, Klagge?' muttered Michener hoarsely. 'You got a touch of religion? Ain't like you to haul off and stop one of your hoodlums from shootin' a man down in cold blood.'

Klagge's face was suffused with a red stain of wrath but he held his temper in check. 'Don't get me wrong, Michener. You're goin' to be taught a lesson, but I'm no fool. I figure maybe I should let Rand take care of you. After he's finished, you might even be pleadin' for death by a bullet.'

Reluctantly, Ford let his right hand drop to his side. He stepped away from the table as Jose Rand got to his feet and shambled forward. Rand, for all his Mexican ancestry, was a hulking brute of a man, totally unlike the slender, dark-haired swarthy-faced man from south of the Texas border. Michener kept his eyes on Klagge, his face tight and cold, eyes narrowed down, determined not to show any fear in front of the other. Perhaps this situation was all his own fault. He should have stayed where he was, at the bar, and taken no heed of what Klagge said. But that would have made no difference, he thought grimly: the other had been determined to bait him, to force the situation to this explosion point, no matter how events had gone.

'You want me to just make sure he won't give us any more trouble?' asked Rand, hands cocked into huge fists.

'That's right,' Klagge said easily, almost disinterestedly, as if he had already put the incident from his mind. He lifted his eyelids a moment, smiling up at Michener. 'I'd warn those two men of yours at the bar not to try to horn in on this, Michener, unless they want to stop a bullet.' He inclined his head a little to where Tom Felder sat, his legs crossed in front of him. There was a Colt in his hand — Michener had not seen him draw it — and it was pointed straight at Carruthers and Denver with Felder's finger hard on the trigger.

Michener felt the tightness build up

swiftly in the pit of his stomach. Suddenly it came to him that there wasn't anything more to be said because Klagge had handed it to Rand and he was no talker. With a man such as this, there was scarcely any time in which to think. In spite of his considerable bulk, the other was as fast as a cat. He came in swiftly, moving forward balanced on the soles of his feet.

Squaring up, Michener side-stepped, swung his fist. Rand saw the blow coming, rolled head and shoulders a little to one side, but Michener shifted his stance in the same fluid movement, brought in his left, catching the bigger man on the side of the face. Pain jarred redly along his hand and wrist as the blow connected, but the other's head snapped back on his neck and he was forced to give ground a little, covering up hastily.

Michener felt a sudden sense of elation, edged forward, swinging again as the other's chin was exposed for a second, but it was another feint on the other's part and his confidence proved to be his undoing. The big fist came from somewhere and crashed against the side of his temple. Arms flailing helplessly, he staggered back, losing consciousness for a second as the force of the blow roared right up into his brain. Through the wavering haze in front of his eyes, he could just make out the sneering grin on Rand's face as he moved in for the kill.

Fighting to retain a hold on his buckling consciousness, he moved away from the other, keeping his guard up more by instinct than anything else, striving to ride the hail of blows which landed with a crushing force on his arms and shoulders, numbing his flesh but doing little damage otherwise. Gradually his breathing eased and he was able to see clearly again. There was still the ringing inside his skull, but he could bear that. He swung right and left, forcing Rand to back off, but only for a little while. Grinning viciously, the other bored in, absorbing the blows to his face and stomach as he closed in.

Crowding in, Rand missed with a short left jab, but connected solidly with his right, hurling Michener back, spinning him round a little so that he staggered against the edge of one of the empty tables. The sharp rim struck him in the small of the back, just on the kidneys, and the pain in his body sent all of the air whistling out of his lungs, clouding his mind once more, leaving him virtually helpless in the face of the other's savage onslaught.

Desperately he tried to cover himself; but most of his strength seemed to have been drained from his body, and Rand hammered strongly through his guard, bunched fist smashing into his stomach. Nausea swept over him in an enervating wave. Again he fell back and this time, the table gave under his weight. Stepping back, Rand stared down at him through glittering eyes, filled with a feral hate. Then he lifted his foot, swung it hard, catching the fallen man in the side.

Michener grunted in agony. His head fell back on to the smashed table with a sickening thud. He tried to get his hands under him, to push himself up from his supine position, but before he could do so Rand had bent, his fingers curled into Michener's shirt front, holding him up with one hand while he hit him again and again in the face with the other. Each time he did, Michener's head was slapped from side to side and everything began to go furry and hazy in his mind, and it was no longer possible for him to see anything properly at all.

'All right,' said Klagge casually. 'That's enough, Jose. No sense in wastin' any more strength on him. He ain't able to feel a thing now. If this don't teach him the lesson he deserves, then we'll just have to take it up some other day. Take him out and throw him into the alley outside where he belongs. These two *hombres* can take him back to the Lazy T.' He uttered a harsh, derisive laugh, turned back to the card game as if nothing had happened.

Rand bent, hauled Michener's limp body upright, dragged him to the door and thrust him out into the narrow alley that ran alongside the saloon. Then he went back inside, gestured with his thumb to Carruthers and Denver.

'All right,' he muttered. 'Git! You'll find him outside.'

★   ★   ★

For the better part of an hour, Michener lay unconscious. When he finally came to, his body was afire with a mass of pain. Each time he drew in a sobbing breath a stab of red-hot agony seared along the muscles of his chest, biting deeply in towards his heart. He lay quite still for several moments, only vaguely aware of the curious swaying motion as if the ground were heaving and tilting beneath his body. There was the saltiness of clotted blood around his mouth and he tried weakly to lift his head, to spit it out. Only then did he realize that he was not lying on the ground but in a buckboard of some kind. He could feel the roughness of the planed wood beneath his fingers as he attempted to prop himself up on one hand, and the creak of greased axles and leather braces sounded close by in his ear.

Forcing his eyes to stay open, he peered into the darkness all about him. Two dimly seen figures were just visible, etched in silhouette against the moonlit sky, their backs to him. As he moved, pursed his lips and tried to call out, one of them turned, saw that he was conscious and moved back into the rear of the buckboard, kneeling over him.

'What in hell happened?' he mumbled through split lips.

'You got yourself beaten up in the saloon,' Carruthers said harshly. 'It was Klagge and some of his boys. They held a gun on us and Jose Rand did his best to thrash you within an inch of your life. Then he tossed you out into the alley.'

Memory returned in short, painful bursts to Michener. He forced himself to sit up in spite of the throbbing agony in his head as his skull threatened to fly apart, as the blood rushed to his head. Groaning, he flopped a hand across his eyes where even the white moonlight sent prancing spears of pain through his temples. In the moonlight, the results of Jose Rand's attack were pitilessly apparent. He got hold of the wooden upright just behind Denver's back, curled his fingers tightly around it, half hanging on to it, his body slouched, all loose and physically ragged. Through the sodden thickness of his thoughts he was recalling the humiliating indignity of what had happened to him in the saloon. He had ridden into town confident that he could hire men to help him protect the Lazy T against Klagge's men; now he was riding back, a beaten man. The realization was gall in his mind.

'You got any water there?' he grunted.

Carruthers moved back to the front of the buckboard, then came back with a canteen, held it to the other's lips and let it dribble down into his throat. It washed the salty blood from his mouth where some of his teeth seemed to have been either knocked out or loosened under Rand's savage onslaught and, reaching up, he let some of it soothe his beaten head and face. It returned a little of the strength to him and he was able to sit up without support. While he rested there, the full realization of his present position came to him and he writhed with an inner torment and bitterness. Right now, Austen Klagge seemed to be holding all of the cards. He took another pull at the canteen, holding it in both hands, steadier now. Lowering the canteen, he gave a deep, shuddering sigh. Mumbled words spilled across his lips, a man talking to himself, not liking his own thoughts.

'I failed. By God — I failed! Nothin' to stop him movin' in and shootin' down every man I got, drivin' all of the cattle out of the valley and fencin' up the creek all the way along.'

Carruthers squatted there in the moonlit darkness, listening to him, saying nothing, letting him ramble on, not sure whether the other actually meant what he was saying, or whether it was the effect of the beating he had taken. After a while, once he was certain the other had recovered consciousness fully, he left Michener clutching the canteen and crawled back to sit beside Denver on the tongue of the buckboard.

'How is he?' Denver asked softly.

'He'll live,' muttered the other, staring straight ahead of him where the trail was a pale grey scar twisting over the hills. 'But there's nothin' much more he can do. Klagge has him beaten for good.'

It was the quiet time of the early

morning hours when they finally rode into the courtyard of the Lazy T ranch. Shaking off Carruthers's helping hand, Michener stumped towards the porch, his face set in hard lines. He paused for a long moment on the veranda, looked about him out of flat, incurious eyes, then went inside. He did not look back at the two men in the courtyard.

2

Troublebuster

Fresno City was a typical frontier town, unpleasant to the eye and nose, its main street a river of white alkali dust that was hard on a horse's feet, its buildings strewn around in a haphazard fashion as if the place had been thrown up in a single night and no planning at all had gone into its erection. There had been no regard for order when Fresno City had been put up. Frank Corrie pondered this as he stepped off the stage in front of the long-faced hardware store, feeling the stinging dust go down into his throat and lungs with each breath he took. Here and there, tall two- and three-storeyed buildings thrust themselves up above the flat-roofed adobe style buildings where the American influence was beginning to show and oust an earlier Mexican type of building. The older places were faced with paint that hung peeling from the sun-bleached wood and the Mexicans had evidently not bothered about any kind of decoration to their houses, being content to use a flat overall wash of paint which obviously failed to stand up to the endless ravages of sun and sand and time.

The driver dropped his bag down from the box on top and, a few moments later, the stage rolled on around the corner to the depot. Frank turned for a last look at it, scowled as the memory of that long ride across the desert to the east came back to him. Four days in a stage was enough to test any man's endurance. Even on that flat trail through the alkali, its swaying, jolting motion had been enough to turn his stomach. First thing in the morning he determined to get himself a horse. He would always be more at home on a horse than in a stage.

God, what a place! The town was

dirty and made up of harsh, ugly lines, and the stench from the narrow, twisting alleys that opened off at intervals along the main street was composed of garbage and other man-made smells that offended the nostrils of a man used to the sage and the wide-open trails that lay between forests of tall, sweet-scented pine. It was small wonder that the people who lived here all of their days stagnated and became tainted with the same evil and ugliness.

He shifted the heavy bag to his right hand, moved on down the street. The eyes beneath the level brows were a clear grey, had once been direct and full of warmth, but now there were the lines of trouble and weariness etched in the forehead above them and they seemed sunk a little as if they had looked out on the consequence of past acts which had left their mark for good. He smiled grimly to himself. A man found that he always had to harvest the results of his deeds in some form or another. There was a gnawing pang of hunger in his stomach now and he looked about him for a hotel. There was a couple of cantinas on the far side of the street, windows glimmering lustily in the sunlight that flooded over the town. He chose the nearer of the two and went inside. It was a little cooler here than in the street and he sank gratefully into a chair at the table near the window, facing the door. It was an instinctive choice, one he had followed religiously for more years than he cared to remember. Looking at him, nearly six feet tall, his body tapered to a hard leanness, it was hard to realize he was not yet twenty-eight. Trouble had aged him another five years at least.

The room reeked of stale food, tobacco smoke and other indefinable odours he could not place, but his hunger was too insistent for him to notice this. The man who appeared in the open doorway just beyond the counter was of tremendous girth and the greasy apron he wore made him appear even larger. He said: 'It's a little early, *señor.*'

'I'll take anything you've got,' Frank said.

The other nodded and vanished into the room at the back. He returned five minutes later with some hot stew in a bowl, set it in front of him with some bread and black coffee.

The man said anxiously: 'Is it all right, *señor?*'

Frank nodded. 'It's fine.' He ate ravenously. The Mexican remained hovering in the background, watching him.

'You came in on the stage?' asked the other as Frank wiped the plate clean with a piece of bread and picked up the cup of coffee.

'That's right. Four days on the overland stage is more'n enough for any man. I figure on buyin' myself a horse first thing in the mornin'.'

'They have horses for sale at the livery stables just along the main street. Good horses, most of them. But

Fernandez is a rogue, you must be careful buying from him.'

'I reckon I know good horseflesh when I see it,' Frank told him. 'How about gettin' myself a bed for the night? Seems like I'm stuck in this place until tomorrow.'

'There is only one hotel as yet, señor,' murmured the other, his tone apologetic. 'Halfway along the street. This is the middle of the hot season. You'll have no difficulty getting a bed there.'

'Thanks.' Frank finished his drink. 'I'll be on my way there.' He dropped a dollar on to the table, lifted his bag and walked towards the door.

Behind him, the Mexican picked up the dollar, held it tightly in his thick-fingered fist for a long moment as he stared after the man who was now making his way along the dusty street outside. A strange one that, he reflected. He did not quite know what to make of the other. A sad man, one who had known trouble in his life and been marked with it — and yet there was an air of ruthlessness about him that struck a chord in the other's mind and sent a little shiver of nameless fear through him. It had been more than the look in the stranger's eyes which had done this, more than the lithe, catlike way in which he walked.

It had been the gun tied down low on his hip, the black butt worn smooth from long and constant use. Felipe had seen men come and go in Fresno City. He knew a gunfighter when he saw one. And he knew also that if this man intended to stay in town, there would be trouble with a mighty big T let loose in the territory before long.

★ ★ ★

He walked a hundred yards and then made out the sign over a three-storey building which said FRESNO HOTEL. The building stood out from most of the others which clustered haphazardly about it and it had an air of solidity which the others lacked, as if it had been built to last. Crossing the dusty street, he went inside.

There was an unaccustomed silence in the building and he reckoned the Mexican had been right when he had claimed the place would be virtually empty at this time of year. A short, sallow-faced man sat behind the desk at the end of the lobby. He eyed Frank appraisingly as he walked forward.

Corrie asked: 'Can I get a room here for the night?'

'Guess you can take your pick, mister,' said the other genially. 'Nobody staying here right now. Reckon we won't have any visitors for another month or so until the rains come.' He got to his feet and peered forward as Frank signed the register.

'Frank Corrie, eh?' he muttered. Turning, he took down a key and handed it across the desk. 'At the end once you get to the top of the stairs.

Best room we got in the hotel. That'll be two dollars, ten cents more if you want a bath.'

'I sure could use one after bein' on that stage.'

'Have the swamper draw the water for you in half an hour. Give you a call when it's ready.'

Turning the key in the lock, Frank went inside the room. It was sparsely furnished, with a low iron bed, a chest of drawers over by the window, a small table and a couple of chairs. Situated where it was, the sun had been beating down on that particular wall of the hotel for most of the day and the heat in the room was stifling. He hastily threw open the window, stuck in the nail which held it up and let some air into the room.

The bare condition of the room meant little to him. He had been used to such places for a long time now among the frontier towns from Memphis all the way out here. Tomorrow he would be riding on, seeking to fulfil the restless urge that bubbled up inside him these days.

Taking off his boots, he stretched himself out on the bed, forced his weary bones and muscles to relax. He was half-asleep when the knock came at the door. Opening it, he found the clerk there.

'Your bath's ready, Mister Corrie.'

He followed the other down the stairs into the small room at the back and allowed himself the luxury of a good soaking in the hot, steamy water which had been poured into the long tin bath for him.

* * *

It was still dark when he woke the next morning, but through the window, off to the east, he could just make out a thin bar of silver spread over the horizon. Pulling on his boots, he went to the window and looked out. Even in the first pale glimmerings of an early dawn, the town had lost none of its

46

inborn ugliness. Here and there he could see the newly erected buildings, picked out by the bright newness of the wooden planks from which they had been constructed.

So very like scores of similar towns he had known in the past ten years, thrown up by men whose morals were few and whose conscience was a soft and easy thing. Built by men with sweat and guts and gall. Soon, it would either grow or die. Somewhere along the line there would be the turning point for Fresno City, an event which would decree if it would become a great and important city, or if the builders would drift away from it, leaving it empty and utterly deserted, like the ghost towns further to the north where only the tumbleweed gave any movement to the dust-sifted streets that lay like grey rivers between tumbledown buildings of rotting timber and slate.

He ate a quick breakfast in the small cantina along the street, then went along to the livery stables. The short, dark-haired Mexican gave him a quick, appraising glance. From the back of the stalls, he brought out a black bay.

'Thirty dollars,' he said shortly. 'For another five I throw in the saddle and bridle.'

Frank smoothed his hand over the bay's legs and chest, stared into the mouth and then nodded. 'It's a deal,' he said.

He made the cinch tight under the animal's belly, then swung up into the saddle. It was still too early for most of the citizens of Fresno City to be up and about and the street was almost deserted as he rode out, heading north. As he turned the bend in the trail at the far end of town, however, a solitary figure stepped out of the long shadows near the saloon, and walked purposefully towards the livery stables.

Out of small, narrowed eyes, Laredo Ford stared down at the Mexican groom. 'You know that *hombre* who just rode out on the black bay?' he asked. His voice ran rough like gravel.

'No, Señor Ford.' Fernandez shook his head. 'He is a stranger to me.'

'Yet you sold him a horse.'

'He paid me well for it — and the saddle.'

'Hell with that,' cut in the other bleakly. 'Mr Klagge likes to know about every stranger who comes ridin' through Fresno City. He won't like it if he hears you sold a mount and didn't find out anythin'.'

'His name is Frank Corrie,' said Fernandez hurriedly. A dismal understanding came to him. He recognized the signs only too clearly. Ford was out to make trouble and nothing he could say would prevent it. He knew only too well the meanness that was in Klagge's hired hands, particularly gunmen such as this one. Still seeking a peaceful solution, he said meekly: 'He spent the night at the hotel after getting into town on the stage. I'm sure they can tell you more about him there.'

'You seem to know plenty if you can only be made to open your mouth. But

49

you Mexs are all alike.'

'I know nothing more, Señor Ford,' protested the other.

Ford moved closer, menacingly. 'You don't seem to understand the position. I said I want to know who he is, not just his name. Looked too much like a gunfighter to me.'

'Why should a gunfighter ride into Fresno City to buy a horse?' inquired the Mexican innocently.

Ford's open hand slashed viciously across his face, jerking his head back on his neck. Fernandez stumbled against one of the stalls, arms lifted in an attempt to protect his face. Laredo Ford was grinning viciously as he swung again, this time to the stomach. Inside the stall the horse there, startled, swung away, kicked out thunderously at the wooden walls. With an effort, Fernandez forced himself upright. His mouth felt swollen and he had the feeling that his nose was broken. Through his wavering vision, he saw the other coming in again, knew that nothing was going to stop the gunhawk.

His flailing arm caught at the side of the stall. There was a long-handled quirt hanging there, used whenever any of the horses got fractious. It wasn't much use against a man at this range, but the handle was shot loaded and, almost without thinking, angered and half-blinded by the pain in his head, he grabbed at it, reversing it with his fingers, lashing out at Ford as the other man came in.

The full weight of the weapon did not connect solidly, the whip handle glancing down the right side of Ford's head. Even so, it rocked the bigger man by the unexpectedness of it, sending him back on his heels. A thin trickle of blood oozed slowly down Laredo's cheek from beneath the brim of his hat. For a second he stood there, swaying a little, putting up his hand to his head and peering in half-bewildered surprise at the smear of blood on the back of his fingers. He uttered a savage roar, drawing his gun. Through half-closed

51

eyes, Fernandez saw the barrel lifted, lining up on his chest. He saw the round black hole like an empty, evil eye staring at him, chilling the blood in his veins. He saw the gunman's finger tighten on the trigger, the knuckles gleaming white for a split second before the brief flash of flame from the muzzle. Something slammed hard into his chest, hurling him back into the door of the stall, the force of it holding him there for a few moments, arms and legs spread in an attitude of crucifixion. Then his legs bent and he started down in a loose, slithering fall.

Staring down at the limp body of the man he had just killed, Laredo Ford pulled his lips back flat across his teeth. The pale eyes still burned with the lust to kill. He lowered the gun and, in his spasm of hate, he wanted to pump slug after slug into the sprawled body but, with an effort, he conquered the feeling, twisted his head sharply and peered about him with a wolfish wariness. That gunshot would have been heard by someone, early as it was, and he did not want to find himself on a murder charge. With reluctant slowness, he lowered the gun, releasing the cocked hammer cautiously, and thrust it back into its holster. Then he turned and moved into the pale glimmer of sunlight, cast a quick look up and down the street, and ran for the saloon on the far side, melting into the dark shadows which still lay in the narrow alleys.

Two minutes after he had fled the stables, three men arrived on the scene. Felipe Rodriguez from the cantina got there first and Clem Duprey, the sheriff, and Fent Corday were only moments behind him.

'You see anybody here, Rodriguez?' Duprey asked, bending beside the dead man.

'Nobody, Sheriff. He was lying here when I arrived.'

'I saw a rider spurring away from the stables about the time of the shot, Sheriff,' put in Corday. 'I'd just come out of my office.'

'You recognize him?'

'Stranger to me. He was riding the big black bay.'

'Only man it could have been would be that *hombre* who stayed at the hotel last night,' put in Felipe quickly. His eyes gleamed. 'He rode in on the stage yesterday afternoon, came into the cantina for a bite to eat, and then went over to the hotel. He told me he meant to buy a horse and ride out first thing this morning.'

Duprey straightened up, his face set in grim, hard lines. 'Looks like he's the killer,' he allowed, after a pause. 'Better get the undertaker here, Fent. Meantime, I'll have a word at the hotel and then get a posse together.' He rubbed a thoughtful hand over his chin. 'Won't be easy followin' his trail on that hard ground yonder, specially if he does his best to cover it. Pity there's been no rain to soften the ground.'

Turning sharply on his heel, he made his way to the hotel. The clerk gave him a faint look of surprise which deepened as the sheriff explained his presence.

'Why certainly he stayed here, Sheriff,' he said crisply. His tone grew more confiding. 'I knew there was something about that man as soon as he walked in. He looked like a gunhawk, and that gun of his gave him away.'

Duprey stared down at the signature in the register. 'Frank Corrie,' he said musingly. In his mind's eye, he pictured all of the Wanted notices he had stacked away in his office desk, not that this told him much. It was easy for a killer to change his name with every town he visited. The description which the clerk could give him did not fit with any of the pictures he had, but that, too, was no guarantee that this stranger who called himself Frank Corrie was not a wanted man. The stretches of territory along the frontier harboured many criminals always staying one jump ahead of the law. It was that which made his job more difficult than it need be.

'You reckon he's the man who killed

Fernandez, Sheriff?' asked the clerk, when he had given all the information he had to offer.

'Right now, it sure looks that way.'

The other's gaze was puzzled. 'He looked like a man who knows how to handle a gun,' agreed the clerk. 'But why should he gun down Fernandez in cold blood like that? Who'd want to kill a man just for a horse?'

Duprey shrugged. 'Ain't no concern of mine why he did it,' he retorted harshly. 'All that concerns me now is bringin' him in for trial. If he's innocent, then he'll have his chance to prove it in front of a judge.'

★   ★   ★

Frank Corrie had been riding through thickly timbered ground during most of the morning and now, with the sun lifting its noon zenith, he came out of the tall pines and found himself looking down on to the desert that stretched away to the south. The trail he had been following from Fresno City dipped down through a rock-strewn glade and wound down past a scatter of tumbled boulders into the white, sun-glaring alkali.

He considered the prospect of riding out into the Badlands in the full glare and heat of the high noon sun, found it not to his liking, and swung off the trail, back towards the trees, riding on until he found a sun-glinting ellipse of water surrounded by thick, ankle-deep grass which would make a good nooning place.

Although he knew little of the bay, he saw at once by the way it drank deeply from the waterhole, its muzzle buried deep beneath the surface of the water all the time, that it was a thoroughbred and unlikely to roam far if he left it unreined. Unsaddling, he turned the horse loose, reins dragging on the ground, and stretched himself out in the shadow of a solitary redwood. He had a little food in his saddleroll and he ate slowly, chewing on it contemplatively. Gradually he felt a little better, as if he were part of something huge and good that enveloped the whole of this part of creation and the past affairs of his life seemed of little real consequence, almost as if they had happened to some other man.

Stretching himself out in the shade of the tree, he tilted his wide-brimmed hat over his eyes, feeling the warmth of the sun on his body. Judging by the way it soon glinted on his face, shining almost directly into his eyes, he must have fallen asleep.

Pushing himself to his feet, he moved over to where the horse stood hipshot within a couple of yards of the pool. The sun was down a little but there was boiling heat still in the air and no promise of any coolness to come. Swinging up into the saddle, he headed out into the desert. Inferno air swirled about him. On the distant horizons and even nearer at hand, the dust devils lifted and eddied. A rattler, wakened from its sleepy state, slid towards the shade of an upthrusting rock and the horse shied a little at the sudden movement. Elsewhere there was only the flashing, darting purple-backed sand lizards showing movement and colour to the flat, featureless desert.

There was the shadowy smudge of fresh vegetation on the skyline, on the further edge of the desert, but it was a good ten miles to it and Frank resigned himself to a long and uncomfortable ride. Early afternoon heat was a settled and heavy burning weight across his back and shoulders, and he instinctively tipped his head forward against the unyielding pressure of it. He felt a brush of impatience in his mind at the slowness of the sun's horizon-ward movement, wishing for the time when it would have sunk into dark obscurity beyond the purple-shimmering hills in the far west.

These blazing-white alkali ridges made a parched and tortured land and when, an hour later, he came on the dried-out bed of a river, the pebbled bed scrabbed and ugly with cracked clay and scum, with only a few pools left here and there, the full enormity of the drought which had come to this part of the territory was brought home to him. Small wonder that the ranchers hereabouts were finding it difficult to make ends meet. The cattle must be dying by the hundred for lack of water.

He came on to the narrow stretch of sage and mesquite some time around five o'clock, with the terrain losing some of its monotonous flatness, lifting towards the low foothills. It had been hard riding during the sun-blasted heat of the long afternoon. Hard and mean. His dusty clothing was sticking to his body from the sweat that had lashed from every pore and he felt like a board that had lain out too long in the sun, becoming warped and brittle.

His mount made slow and painful progress through the sharp-edged leaves of the Spanish Sword, picking its way cautiously forward. Gradually, however, the land changed. There were low bushes at first and then, some three hundred yards away, trees lifted from a tangled mass of underbrush and he guessed there was water there. His stomach signalled its hunger by setting up a churning clamour and he gigged the bay forward, anxious to reach the creek he reckoned lay directly ahead of him. This would be the edge of some fairly big spread, he guessed, and it was just possible he might get some food and a bed for the night.

Moments later he heard the sharp sound that came from directly in front of him and instinct made him slacken his mount's progress as he lifted himself a little in the saddle.

He recognized the sound at once. Somebody was chopping wood with an axe, using slow, powerful strokes.

Caution made him rein up a moment later and slip from the saddle. There was a narrow trail some ten yards away and he followed it, crouching down as he moved forward. Reaching a low rise, he slithered to the top of it, parted the branches of the bushes which grew on the crest. There was a small clearing perhaps fifty yards away. Beyond it the creek glinted in the bright sunlight. The sun glinted too on the wire strung between the posts that had been hammered firmly into the ground. Everything lay hot and still under the powerful drive of the sun. Then came movement a little to his right.

A man emerged from the brush, swinging the heavy, long-handled axe in his right hand. Pausing to spit on his hands, he bent and attacked one of the posts, the sharp edge of the blade biting deeply into the stout wooden post, sending the chips flying over his shoulder. Three minutes later the oak had been bitten right through and a length of the fence collapsed.

Straightening, the man wiped the back of his hand across his forehead, the axe resting against one leg. Frank grinned, relaxed. He was not sure why this fence had to come down, but he doubted if there was any danger associated with this man. He was on the point of getting to his feet when the rifle shot bucketed through the clinging stillness, jarring on his ears. One shot — but it leapt against the silence like a live thing and through the heat haze Frank saw the man in the clearing suddenly jerk and slump as the slug took him in the back. Swiftly, Frank crouched down, jerking the Colt from its holster. He caught a brief glimpse of the small rift of smoke drifting in the still air from above the bushes on the far side of the clearing. Frank felt his nerves tingle. In an instant he was down behind the low rise, worming his way around, through the cluster of rocks, circling to bring himself around behind the bushwhacker.

Evidently there was only one gunman among the bushes since only one shot had been fired. Wriggling back down a narrow gully, he crawled through a cactus thicket where he could run unseen provided he kept his head well down. Then he set out on the wide detour, making little noise as he cat-footed through the shifting dust.

Here the ground was in his favour. Another burst of running and scrambling and he dropped safely into a long, trough-like depression that swung around behind the spot where he had noticed that puff of rifle smoke. He paused occasionally to check whether the killer intended coming out of cover to make certain he had killed the man in the clearing, but there was no sign of him. Hauling himself up among the rocks, feeling the hot, burning touch under his fingers, he came up to a place where he could look down on the wide thicket of trees and bushes along the banks of the creek. Over to one side he could see his own horse nibbling at the grass, patiently waiting for him to return. But in all other directions he could see no sign of the killer. It was possible that the other had already decided he had finished the chore he had set out to do and was working his way back to where he had left his own mount. But Frank was not the sort of man to take any unnecessary chances. He stole along the depression, first descending, and then climbing again, and it was as he gained the top of a large flat rock that he caught his first glimpse of the other, more than three hundred yards away, clambering swiftly down a rocky slope, running through the tangle of thorn. He was too far away for a killing shot with a revolver, and Frank's Winchester was back in the saddle.

Reluctantly he thrust the Colt back into its holster, moved back to the clearing. For a murderous moment he was tempted to saddle up and ride out after the other. But a second's contemplation was enough to tell him he did not stand a chance of overtaking the killer. His own mount was footsore after the long ride across the alkali.

For a moment he stood over the man who lay sprawled face-downward on the ground, fingers dug deep into the dirt, twisted in a final spasm of life.

Then he bent and gently turned him over, felt for the pulse in the limp wrist. There was none. The man's eyes were empty and staring, already beginning to glaze. The slug had shattered his spine, must have killed him outright.

There was no sign of the man's horse and, after a moment's contemplation, Frank hauled the body across the clearing and lifted it across his own saddle. He had no idea who the man might be, but it seemed evident that he worked for one of the ranchers close by and the least that could be done for him would be to give him a decent burial.

There was darkness drawing in from the east by the time he had followed the trail over one of the high foothills, down into the lush green valley that lay beyond. He made out the shape of a big house built just beyond a clump of trees, built of stone and hand-hewn timber, and on the far side of it a couple of barns with a bunkhouse nearer at hand off to one side of the courtyard. There was a corral too, with half a dozen fine-looking horses in it. He eyed the place musingly for a moment, noticed the grey smoke that lifted from the chimney.

Pausing for only a moment, he set the bay at the downgrade, rode into the line of trees. There were a few yellow lights just showing through the windows of the ranch house, and for a long moment he experienced that strange sense of nostalgia which came to him at times such as this. It seemed so long since he had known a home, a place to ride home to when the evenings were drawing in, and the first of the sky sentinels were beginning to show in the eastern heavens. Ahead of him was a home for some man, comfort, a place to belong to — all the things, in fact, that a man such as himself would never own.

'All right, hold it right there, mister!'

The harsh command came from among the tangled brush to his left and the horse jerked up its head in sudden fright. Frank's hand whipped down towards his Colt, then he stayed it as the man stepped out into the open, the rifle trained on him. He let the sixgun drop back into its holster and reached forward to soothe the horse.

The man stepped directly into the middle of the trail. He was sharp-featured, eyes fixed unwaveringly on Frank's face. 'What do you want here, mister?' he demanded.

Frank squinted at the other through the gathering gloom, felt a faint sense of relief to see that he was dressed in working garb. 'I figured this man might have worked here,' he said, gesturing towards the body across the saddle. 'I came across him down by the creek to the south of here.'

Warily the other approached, lifted the man's head and peered closely at it. Frank heard his sharp intake of breath. 'It's Clem.' His tone was tight with surprise and disbelief. The barrel of the Winchester lifted a little higher and there was a mean note in his voice. 'Did you kill him, mister?'

Frank shook his head. 'Talk sense,' he muttered. 'If I'd killed him, would I be totin' his body around lookin' for somebody who owns him?'

The other was clearly a man of limited imagination, but he finally shook his head. 'Reckon not, stranger. But I figure you'd better get down off that bay and walk along to the ranch with me. The boss will want to ask a few questions.'

'Suits me.' Frank slid from the saddle, walked slowly beside the bay down the trail with the ranch hand walking a few feet behind, still covering him with the rifle, still unsure of him.

When they emerged from the trees into the courtyard, the man gave a quick shout. Two men came out of the bunkhouse in response to the yell and, a moment later, the door on the porch opened and a tall man, silhouetted against the yellow glow, stood there.

'What's wrong out there, Charlie?'

'*Hombre* just rode in with Clem's

body, Mister Michener,' Charlie called back.

Michener stepped down into the yard, came forward with the two men from the bunkhouse behind him. He got directly in front of Frank, who moved a few feet away from the bay. Suspicion lay heavy in the taut stillness. Tension held the men tight.

Michener looked at the dead man's face, then searched Frank with a glance that believed nothing. Even from that look, Frank guessed how things were in this part of the territory. He had felt a little of it in town. Here it was stronger still. There was a range war brewing, he felt certain of that — and unless he was very careful, he might just find himself standing right in the middle of it. He had had past experience of these wars that flared up, often for little enough reason, along the wild and lawless frontiers. A ruthless, power-hungry man wanted to make himself bigger and wealthier than he really was; a few men would be shot, some head of cattle rustled off the range, and before anybody knew what was happening, tempers would flare and what would ensue would bring death and hatred as bad as anything that had been seen during those terrible months and years of the Civil War.

'It's Clem all right,' he said eventually. 'Where'd you find him?'

'Out at the edge of this spread,' said Frank evenly. He dug into his pocket, brought out the makings of a cigarette and rolled the tobacco slowly into the brown paper before placing it between his lips and lighting it. He drew the smoke equally slowly into his lungs, let it out through his parted lips. 'He was shot by some *hombre* hidin' among the trees.'

'Then he wasn't dead when you found him?'

'No. He was smashing down a fence along the creek. I'd just ridden up when the shot was fired. I tried to get the killer but he was too far away. He had a horse among the trees.'

Michener listened to his voice, weighed it. He had started out, like Charlie, cool and suspicious of him, and it seemed he wanted it to remain that way. Still, Frank saw the faint change in his shadowed features, saw a small gust of expression go over his face. His eyes were very still, but in their depths a deep wrath moved slowly. His shoulders slumped just fractionally. 'I reckon you're telling the truth, mister — '

'Frank Corrie. You know who might have killed him?'

The other nodded. Without answering the question, he turned to the two men behind him. 'Take the body into the barn, boys. We'll bury him tomorrow.' He waited until Clem's body had been lifted from the horse, then turned to Frank.

'Where are you headed for, Corrie?'

Frank said: 'I was just ridin' through from town. Got there yesterday on the stage. Either I'll ride on through or stay here if I like it.'

'That means nothing,' murmured the other. He was a solid character, Frank decided, a man with deep convictions, but with something akin to fear now riding him hard. 'There is always somethin' that drives a man to do what he does. You could be on run from somethin'.'

'I could be.'

Michener's face tightened a shade. His gaze grew bright and sharp, calculating.

'You want a job?'

'Doin' what?' Frank countered.

'The usual. Ridin' herd, mendin' fences.'

'You're sure that's what you want?' Frank gave the other a cynical grin. 'From what I saw in town, and now this,' he inclined his head in the direction of the nearby barn into which the dead man had been carried, 'seems to me you want a gunhawk rather than a cowpuncher.'

Michener ceased to smile, gave a terse nod. 'Could be there'll be more

73

shootin' than ridin',' he admitted.

'You afraid of somethin'?'

'Out here along the frontier a man has to defend what he has and in the face of men like Austen Klagge, it means fightin' with everythin' he has at his disposal. Klagge's men are running roughshod over all of this territory. That fence you saw, at the creek. It's on my land. Klagge put it up to try to stop me movin' my own cattle down to the creek for water. Now that this drought has been goin' on for four months, there's precious little water left anywhere around Fresno City. In the past six weeks I've lost three men and five others have been wounded by dry-gulchers. More'n three hundred head of prime beef have been rustled and it won't be long before Klagge decides to stampede his herd across my land to the water.'

'Then why not inform the sheriff and let the law take over?'

'Inform him of what? I've got no proof that it was any of Klagge's men who shot my hands. Duprey is a straight man, but he needs proof, and Klagge has plenty of influence around these parts. It'd be his word against mine.'

'So you figure on hirin' yourself a fast gun and hope to settle things that way?'

Michener shrugged. 'Klagge has hired plenty of gunslingers to do his dirty work for him. Daily men ride into town and join up with him. And there are more gunhawks than cattle hands among 'em.'

Frank drew on his cigarette, the glowing tip a red flare in the dimness. He pondered the other's proposition for a long moment, turning it over in his mind. 'How do you figure I can help you?'

'You look like a man used to handling a gun. The sort of man I need if I'm to fight Klagge.'

'You don't know anythin' about me. Who I really am, or why I'm here.'

'Means nothin' to me,' declared the

other emphatically. 'I ask no questions of any man who works for me. All I demand is loyalty. Of course, if the threat of Klagge is enough to make you want to ride on, then — '

Frank smiled a little. The other was still prying him, he reckoned, trying to gauge his worth and character. He said: 'I wouldn't run because of any man, and I wouldn't stay if I figured you only wanted me to kill for you. But I'll stay for my own reasons.'

The other showed relief; and then the expression of relief faded and he became brisk and to the point again. 'No need to let your reasons out. You'll find a place in the bunkhouse yonder. It's late now. We can have another talk in the morning. Throw your horse into the corral.'

Turning on his heel, Michener walked slowly back to the house. As he left, Frank noticed the slight limp. It went with the deep, purple bruises he had noticed on the rancher's face. Evidently Michener had come up against Klagge and his hirelings recently.

Leading the bay to the corral, he turned it loose and hung the bridle and saddle on one of the stakes before making his way to the bunkhouse. Starlight laid a pale glimmering fire over the heavens now, all the way down the deep purple slopes to the horizon.

Thrusting open the door of the bunkhouse, he walked inside, pegged his saddleroll and found himself a bunk. Sitting on the edge of it, he looked around at the other men there. Distrust showed in some of their eyes and he knew they were seeing the same thing as Michener had noticed at once, even in the gloom. The mark of the gunfighter was written all over him.

3

The Big Frame

Dawn crept slowly into the world in a pale greyness, then became a lavish red and gold as the sun lifted clear of the eastern horizon, promising no relief from the heat and the dryness. The small group of men, headed by Clem Duprey, made a slow ride through the tangled brush along the western border of the Lazy T spread. They had spent most of the previous afternoon trailing the tracks of a lone rider along horse-crippling grades and down shale-treacherous slopes, spending the night making cold camp on the edge of the hills. Now, with the first light of dawn, after losing the trail on several occasions, they were approaching the ranch house.

'Looks like they're already awake,'

commented Sorley, one of the posse. 'You figure he rode here after he left town?'

'Could be,' grunted Duprey. He rode out on to a low rise, stared down into the valley. After a moment he added, 'Looks like a fresh horse down there in the corral.'

'That's the black bay he was ridin'. I'm certain of it.' Corbay leaned forward in his saddle. In a changed tone, he went on: 'I might have guessed he'd ride out here and sign on for Michener.'

'What do you mean by that remark?' inquired Duprey.

'Only that Michener rode into town some time ago, threatened my client, Austen Klagge, that he intended to bring in some gunhawks to start a range war. Clearly this incident speaks for itself.' Grimly, he murmured: 'It would come as no surprise to me if we discover that Michener refuses to let us take him back into town for trial.'

'Reckon we'll see about that.' Duprey's tone was equally grim. 'If I don't get a satisfactory explanation from this *hombre* then he'll come back with us, if I have to draw on every man Michener has.'

They rode down into the courtyard, hauled up in front of the house. Duprey was on the point of getting down when the porch door opened and Michener stepped out. He held a Winchester in his hands, covering the small band of men. The sheriff made a move towards his sidearm, then obviously he thought better of it and allowed his hand to drop away.

'Now don't do anythin' hasty, Kent,' he said calmly. 'You, of all people, should know better than to try to buck the law.'

'You reckon I've got any real concern for the law, seein' the way it helped those other ranchers who tried to hold on to their land when Klagge began to move in?' Michener spat the words out viciously. 'I've got no beef with you,

Sheriff, but I see you're ridin' in bad company.'

'What do you mean?'

'Corday. That double-faced snake who's with you. He's workin' for Klagge. If he's here, then I can figure out for myself that Klagge is somewhere at the back of this little play of yours.'

'This has got nothin' to do with Klagge,' Corday said sharply. 'Now put up that rifle and let's talk this thing out sensibly.'

The barrel of the Winchester did not waver by so much as an inch. 'You can say what you have on your mind from there, Clem. Then I'll ask you to ride on. I want no more trouble with Klagge, but if he tries anythin' more, he'll find he's bitten off more'n he can chew.'

'Meanin' that you've already hired this killer, Corrie,' put in Corday smoothly.

'I've hired a man who rode in last night and his name is Corrie,' acknowledged the other stiffly. 'Whether or not he's a killer is no concern of mine. Not so long as there are men ridin' for Klagge who shoot my hired hands down from cover. Corrie rode in last night with Clem Relton's body. He'd been dry-gulched near the creek, shot in the back. I don't see you ridin' out after his killer, or the men who shot the rest of my boys.'

'That does not defend your action in protectin' a murderer,' said Corday blandly.

'Seems to me you're pretty sure of your facts, mister.' Frank stepped into sight around the corner of the house. 'Just who am I supposed to have killed?'

'You Frank Corrie?' Duprey spoke before the lawyer could answer.

'That's right.'

'That your horse in the corral yonder? The black bay?'

'Sure — what of it?'

'You bought him from the livery stables in Fresno City yesterday mornin',' went on Duprey unhurriedly. 'From a man named Fernandez. You were seen goin' into the stables and ridin' out on the bay a little while later. Durin' that time Fernandez was shot down in cold blood.'

'I know nothin' about that,' Frank said flatly.

'Naturally you're goin' to say that,' put in Corday. 'We didn't expect you to admit to his murder. But I saw you myself, riding hell for leather away from the stables just after the shot was fired.'

'Then you're a liar, mister. That groom was alive when I left him. If you searched his clothing you'd have found the money I gave him for the bay. It ain't likely I'd shoot him down and leave that. Besides, I'd no cause to kill him. I never saw him before in my life.'

'How do we know that?' countered the lawyer. 'Killers ride into a frontier town, hell-bent for revenge, seeking out some man they've been huntin' down, shoot him without giving him a chance to defend himself and ride on out again. It happens every day in these frontier cow-towns. We've only got your word for it that you didn't know him.'

'Meanin' that my word ain't good enough?'

'Not for me,' said Duprey. He turned his glance from Frank and stared directly at Michener. 'Now see here, Kent. If you try to obstruct the law, then you'll have to take the consequences. As far as I see it, we've got a case for takin' in this *hombre* on suspicion of murder. If he's innocent, then he'll have his chance to speak out at the trial. If he's guilty, then the sooner we stretch him on the end of a rope, the better. I can understand your feelings about those men you've had killed and if you get any evidence at all to show who did it, then you know I'll act on it, even if they are Klagge's men.'

Frank saw Michener hesitate, saw the barrel of the Winchester lower. But Corday did not hesitate. As soon as the rifle was pointed away from him, his right hand whipped downward, pulled the small derringer from a hidden holster beneath his arm, holding it so that it covered both the rancher and Frank.

'That's better. Now get your horse and ride back with us, Corrie, otherwise I'll be forced to use this.'

'Put up that gun, Corday,' snapped Duprey. 'I'm still in charge here.'

'Just want to be sure that danged old fool doesn't do anything stupid with that rifle,' said the lawyer. He still kept the derringer pointed at the two men.

Duprey bit down his reply. 'All right, Corrie,' he said, tightly. 'Drop your gunbelt and step this way.'

For a moment Frank felt a wave of anger go through him. 'This is the sweetest frame I've ever seen,' he said bitterly. 'You must be goddamn gullible to believe what this man says. I don't know why he's lying about seein' me ride off after that shot had been fired. Maybe he's the murderer himself and — '

'That's one thing I don't believe, Corrie,' said the sheriff, coldly. 'Now unbuckle that gunbelt. I'll give you ten seconds. After that you'll be resistin' arrest and anythin' can happen.'

'*I doubt that, Sheriff*!'

Frank turned his head sharply in sudden astonishment. The girl stood on the porch, her face half-hidden by one of the wooden beams. There was a heavy Colt in her right hand and she faced the mounted men defiantly.

Corday swung his glance in her direction. For a moment the thought of action, of using the derringer in his hand, was visible in his eyes and the set of his jaw. Then he thought better of it, and lowered the gun reluctantly.

'You stay out of this, Miss Stella,' Duprey said. 'This man may be a killer. All I aim to do is take him back with me and lock him up in the town jail until the circuit judge comes around and we can hold a trial.'

'Of course.' There was a little snap in Stella Michener's voice 'I can just guess what kind of trial he'd get. Oh, I'm not blaming you, Sheriff. From what I hear, you're straight enough, but there are others in Fresno City who can bring pressure to bear, and I seriously doubt if this man will live to stand trial once you take him into town.'

'I guarantee his safety myself, Miss Stella,' said Duprey, tightly. He looked nervous and a little uneasy, not sure of her. A man with a gun he could understand and handle, but a woman was a very different matter.

'Maybe the sheriff is right, Stella,' said Michener tiredly. 'We have to allow the law to take charge here. If you like I'll ride into town with them to see for myself and — '

'No!' Stella Michener stepped down into the whitedusted courtyard. She jerked the heavy Colt decisively. 'Ride on out of here — all of you.'

For a long moment Duprey stared down at her. Then he shrugged, wheeled his mount and led the posse out of the courtyard, back along the trail that wound over the hill. Slowly the dust began to settle.

'Thanks for what you did, Miss

Stella,' Frank said quietly. 'It look a lot of courage to stand up to those men.'

'Nonsense!' Her voice was distant, almost aloof. 'They're all sheep. They do exactly what one does.' Her glance ran over his face and a flicker of expression came to her eyes and lips. 'You're not the usual kind of brush jumper. Maybe you're running away from something. Most likely you are. But if you are innocent of Fernandez's killing, then there's someone in Fresno City who sure wants to see you hang and he'll stop at nothing until you are swinging from the end of a rope. Besides, whatever you are, we need you here. My father must have told you something of our present troubles. Klagge is determined to take over our ranch and land. If he can't do it by legal means, then he'll continue killing our men, taking our cattle and then, if everything else fails, he'll drive his herd, all fifty thousand of them, on to our range to take all of the grass and water. If that happens, we're finished.'

Frank gave a brief nod. He was trying to judge her and having a poor time of it. She had altered towards him, had thrown most of his reasoning out of line. Now he tried to re-establish her in the entire scheme of things. There was no doubt that she was as determined a person as her father, possibly more so considering the stand she had just taken with those men: defying the law. He studied her over a thoughtful interval.

Then he hitched his gunbelt higher about his middle, said: 'Reckon I'd better start earnin' my keep.' He glanced at Michener. 'Anythin' special you want me to do today?'

Michener seemed to shake himself, jerking his mind out of some private reverie. For a moment he stared at Frank as if seeing him for the first time, neither interested nor disinterested. He lifted his left hand and made a stiff, sideways jerk with it. 'I need the rest of that fence taken down, the one where you found Clem. Ride out and finish the job. But keep your eyes open.

Klagge won't stop at killing Clem. Once Corday gets back to Fresno City with the news that you're here working for me, he'll pull out everythin' to kill you.'

'I'll be careful,' Frank said. He whistled up his mount from the corral. As he saddled up and rode out, he glanced back over his shoulder. Kent Michener was a troubled and distant spirit, lost in thought. The girl was still standing near the porch rail, watching him curiously, a spark of interest in her eyes. Her expression was unreadable.

Once out of sight of the valley, Frank rode slowly, scanning the ground for any sign of the posse's passage. He judged it to be near a couple of miles before he found where they had swung abruptly off the main trail and cut away to the south, in the direction he was travelling. Idly, he speculated on why they should have done this rather than heading straight back for town. If they had swung around so as to come upon the Lazy T ranch from another direction and take everyone by surprise, it might explain things. He followed the trail for another mile or so before the ground became too hard and rocky for anyone but an Apache to find trail there on the bare rock. It was difficult to tell always what motivated these men. Duprey had seemed to be an honest and dedicated lawman following the dictates of his own conscience. It was relatively rare to find a lawman of his particular breed in a 'place like this; and he had the feeling that Klagge was finding it a disadvantage having a straight-shooting sheriff round.

This would be a punishing day for horses and he allowed the bay to pick its own pace. Ahead of him the ground lifted steeply and within minutes he was picking his way cautiously along a narrow, steep-sided draw, the rough walls closing in on him from both sides. Tension rode with him. He grew increasingly anxious as the canyon extended onward with no sign of the walls dipping, or the draw opening out.

There was just the chance that those men riding with the sheriff were waiting for him, may even have had a man out watching from some convenient spot to keep a check on him, knowing he would have to leave the ranch sooner or later if he was working for Michener.

He sat impatiently forward in the saddle, feeling the hot touch of the sun on his neck and shoulders. It was too hot for comfort and the heat reflected down from the rocks came through his shirt and jacket until it was almost unbearable.

Then, just as the valley showed signs of widening in front of him, he heard the sound of many hoofbeats. Cocking his head on one side, he listened intently. Seconds later he could hear the heavy rumbling of wagon wheels on the rocky ground and the creak of leather braces. The racket made by the wagon slowly increased in volume, moving up from behind him and a little off to one side. Frank felt a momentary uneasiness. Where was that wagon? Was it one of Michener's? It seemed doubtful that Klagge should have a wagon on this stretch of territory, knowing how vulnerable it would be. A fast-riding group of gunmen was one thing; a slow, lumbering wagon another.

He came to an immediate decision. Spurring his mount forward, he rode out into the open, jerking the Colt from its holster. There was a wide, well-used trail some fifty yards away, one which ran alongside the top of the draw. He took in everything in a single glance, lined up the Colt on the man seated on the tongue of the wagon, a short, tousled-hair man who jerked hard on the reins the instant Frank appeared before him, hauling the team of horses to a sliding halt.

The man was about six feet tall, nothing but skin and bone, with the rounded shoulders of a man used to watching the trail continually whether he walked or rode. His eyes were a watery blue, wide open now as they stared at Frank.

'Hold it there, old-timer,' Frank said sharply. 'Who are you and what are you doin' on this part of the trail?'

'Reckon I might ask you the same thing, young fella.'

'I'm Frank Corrie. I work for Kent Michener.'

'Do you now?' The other took a wad of chewing tobacco from his bulging pocket, bit off a piece with a powerful wrench of his teeth and chewed it reflectively. 'Since when?'

'Since last night.'

'Guess that explains it, then,' muttered the other enigmatically.

'Explains what?' Frank lowered the gun a little. There seemed to be nothing to fear from the other, but still one could never be sure. Appearances often tended to be extremely deceptive as many a man had found to his cost, earning a permanent resting place for himself in Boot Hill because of it.

'Why I ain't seen you around before.' He spat tobacco juice into the dirt beside the wagon in a long brown stream. 'I'm Ned Dryer, work for Michener, too.'

'You seen anythin' of a posse ridin' this trail, Ned?' he asked as he holstered the Colt.

The other shook his head. 'Ain't seen nobody since I lit out of the line camp at first light.' He shrugged. 'You in trouble, Frank?'

'Could be.' He explained briefly what had transpired that morning back at the ranch. When he had finished, Dryer gave a nod of his head, his eyes shrewd.

'Sounds like you've run foul of Klagge. He's a mean cuss, that one. Wants to take over the whole range for himself. Not only that, but he's got his own troubles, with very little water on his own spread to keep all his cattle alive until the rains come.'

'I guess I know how to take care of myself. You know about Clem?'

'Nope.'

'Found his body at the creek. He was shot in the back by some coyote. I took his body back to the ranch.'

'Hell-damn,' grunted the caper. ' 'Tain't no wonder some of the boys are takin' their wages and ridin' out. Can't blame 'em.'

Frank cut short the other's reminiscences. 'What you got in the wagon, Ned? Anythin' Klagge would like to get his hands on?'

'Just supplies for the other line camp. I take 'em along each week. Ain't no use to Klagge. Besides, I'm too old a cuss for him to bother about.'

'I wouldn't be too sure about that. He seems set to finish off every man he can. If he can stop the supplies gettin' through, he might push the rest of the men to breakin' point. Mind if I ride with you part of the way?'

'Help yourself. Always glad of company on the trail. Gets a mite lonesome at times.'

The four horses strained forward as Ned laid the lash of the whip over their sweating backs. Protestingly, the wheels turned and the wagon moved joltingly forward. The slope was uneven now, with mottling outcrops of rough stone and, more and more, the forest pressed in on them from both sides before claiming the entire crest of the hill which lifted before them, just beyond the place where the wide trail swung steeply downward.

Riding forward, still uneasy and cautious, Frank scouted the trees ahead of them as best he could. But this was deep woods, with a thick, almost impenetrable undergrowth wrapped around the broad trunks of the pines and a carpet-like layer of needles which had fallen over the years.

Any man, so long as he was alert and wary, could easily avoid being seen from the edges of the trail by keeping well back among the maze of trunks and greenery.

Seated on the tongue of the wagon, Ned seemed totally unconcerned, unlike Frank. There was that faint, but imperceptible itch between his shoulder blades, the feeling that he was being watched closely from somewhere nearby and that there was a rifle laid on him, with an itchy finger on the trigger.

He hoped inwardly that he was mistaken, because this made an ideal spot for an ambush, but he did not think he was. The sensation was an unpleasant one which he had experienced on several occasions and each time it had never let him down. The double file of horses pulled the heavily loaded wagon slowly up the slope, wheels churning up the dry dust until it formed a hazy white cloud around them.

Through the green wall of trees he was able to make out the towering shape of a butte that lay off to the right of the trail. From that distance it looked unscalable, the face was sheer rock but it could well have a smoothly sloping approach on the far side, out of sight from there. Now, if someone was up there, watching the trail, they had only to —

A rifle shot rang out with a shocking abruptness, the harsh bark shattering the stillness into a thousand screaming fragments as the echoes chased themselves away into atrophying crashes of sound, booming from one rock face to the other. The ricochet screeched its banshee wail in his ears in the same instant that he pulled his mount's head sharply around.

Ned half-rose from his seat, his jaw dropping slackly open. Then he hauled savagely on the reins, brought the team to a halt and grabbed for the ancient Springfield in the saddle pouch.

'Goddamn fool,' he rasped. 'He's just givin' himself away. I don't get it.'

The rifle cracked once more and this time the slug found its mark, drawing a bleeding red furrow along the hide of one of the lead horses. It whinnied loudly, plunged viciously in its harness, going down on to its forelegs before straightening up once more.

'Hell!' roared Ned sharply. 'He's aimin' for the horses.'

'Get the team under cover,' Frank yelled. 'And keep your head down.' He side-stepped the bay into the trees, swung swiftly from the saddle and ran at a low crouch into the brush, dropping to his knees as he searched for their hidden assailant. His line of vision was too hampered by the encroaching trees. Edging forward, he took off his hat, found a stick and balanced it on the end of it, pushing it forward until it was clear of the bushes. There was no answering shot and he drew it back a moment later, trying to puzzle out the reason behind this attack. The marksman had been able to draw a good bead on the horses as shown by the accuracy of his second shot, so the range was not too extreme for a rifle. So why had he not first tried for the two men riding with the supply wagon?

It was something he could not answer at that moment and he peered about him, studying his situation. By now, Ned had pulled the team into the shadow of the trees on the far side of the trail and, off to his own right, the track wound into the darker country where the underbrush was even more dense. But the rifle shots had come from beyond that narrow fringe of vegetation. Creeping a couple of yards along the trail, he risked another quick look. He estimated that the rim of the butte was the best part of six hundred yards away, a goodly distance for a rifle shot but, even at that range, it did not need an expert to hit a four-horse team. Moments later he saw a man step into sight on the very brink of the butte, fire a quick shot that scattered along the gravel floor of the valley, and disappear into scattered brush and scrub timber.

Frank did not recognize the other, but it took little imagination to know it was most likely one of Klagge's men. That meant there could also be another around some place, close by, waiting to move in once the man on the butte had drawn away any opposition.

He looked up swiftly as the sound of gunfire came again; two shots from the rifle on the slopes and a heavier, closer sound. Springfield, he thought. Ned's on to him, keeping him pinned down. He edged back to his mount, drew his Winchester from its scabbard and turned back. His eyes caught a momentary movement in the lower pines on the other side of the trail less than fifty yards away.

Got him! he thought tightly. So he had been right in his surmise after all. The second man was close to the trail now, had been very close all the time, and now he was edging closer, ready to take over the wagon while he and Ned were busy with his companion on the butte. Carefully, Frank raised the Winchester, waiting, his finger taut on the trigger.

There!

The figure darted across an open space between a couple of clumps of trees, running crouched low. The sound of the Springfield came again from near the wagon, but Ned had clearly not seen the new danger, had been firing up at the figure on the butte. The man up there was becoming more and more daring now, deliberately showing himself at frequent intervals to draw their fire. Frank decided to put him out of his mind for the time being, concentrating on the other coyote among the trees.

Frank had not pulled the trigger even though the rifle had been trained on the shoulders of the running man. He wanted the other alive if possible. That was the only way they were ever going to pin anything definite on Klagge, anything that would stick as far as the sheriff was concerned. But if I can get across the trail without being seen, I've got him, Frank thought, looking directly at the green tangle where the other had disappeared. Now I know where he is . . . and all I have to do now is go in and get him, or wait until he comes out into the open, becomes over-confident.

He examined the terrain thoughtfully. He was slightly higher than the other, and beyond the cluster of trees there appeared to be more open, rocky ground. Probably, Frank thought, that's how he managed to get there so quickly. He must have crawled up that slope, getting into position among the trees just before the wagon moved along the top of the ravine. The other would not want to cross the open stretch of the trail, even where it was only three or four yards in width. Not now that he and Ned had been alerted. The trees and undergrowth would give him protection until he reached a spot fifteen yards from the wagon where it had been hauled off the trail. So his best bet was to crawl through the brush until he reached that spot and try to pick them off from there. All of this went through Frank's mind in the few seconds before he reached a decision.

Getting his legs under him, he darted across the trail, threw himself down into the tangle of thorn on the far side. There came the bark of the Winchester from the butte and the thin screech of a ricochet whined in his ears and he felt the wind of its passing as he clawed himself forward under cover. He exhaled, face pressed close to the ground.

Crawling along into the brush, he paused and lifted his head cautiously, watching the gunman's position from a different angle. But he could not see the other from there. For the second time since the unexpected attack, Frank settled himself down to wait. The seconds passed and the tension began to build up. Let the silence work on the other, he thought tightly. Sooner or later he'll make his move and then would be the time to nail him.

Less than three minutes later, with the rifle fire from the butte keeping up its barking roar, there came a crackle in the brush. Frank narrowed his eyes, saw the bushes quiver along the edge of the trail. The man who stepped into view was short and stockily built. He carried a rifle cradled in his arms and, moving forward, he stepped up close to where the wagon stood, coming up on the blind side as far as Ned was concerned. Barking a sudden order, he levelled the rifle on the oldster.

Standing upright, Frank moved out on to the trail behind the man, said sharply: 'Hold it right there! Drop that rifle!'

He saw the other's shoulder muscles tense under the chequered shirt as the man gathered himself for a sudden move. There was a harsh click as Frank thrust the bolt of the Winchester home. The man hesitated for less than a second, then reluctantly loosened his hold on the gun, letting it fall at his feet.

'That's better. Now you're showing some sense.' Frank moved around to face the other. He recognized him as one of the men who had been riding with the posse and the realization was a swift and instinctive warning to him. 'Get over near the wagon.'

The other did as he was told, stood close to the wheel. Ned came out from where he had been crouched behind the wagon, still gripping the Springfield.

'You ever seen this critter around

before, Ned?' Frank asked.

'Sure.' The other nodded reflectively. 'He rides for Klagge. One of his hired gunslingers. Name's Crenton. Up from Abilene, so I hear.'

'Just as I figured. Only thing that worries me now is where are the others? Ain't likely they would've split up, leavin' just these two critters around to watch this trail.'

A bullet spattered against the side of the wagon and a split second later there came the distant report of the rifle. Frank motioned the two men around the back of the wagon. 'He's seen what's happened here and he'll be out for blood soon.'

'We can't stick around here while he stops shooting, Frank. Only thing to do is for one of us to go after him while the other stays here to watch this coyote.'

Frank considered that, nodded quickly. 'You sure you can handle this *hombre*? I figure I know where that critter yonder is likely to head for now he knows we've only got him to take care of.'

Ned gave a brief nod. 'I'll take good care of him, Frank,' he said. There was a bright glitter in his eyes. Frank turned towards the man standing by the wagon. He said thinly: 'I guess Kent Michener will know what to do with you, Crenton. He'll have short shrift for men who killed his hired hands and ran off his cattle.'

Crenton grinned suddenly, a quick grin of triumph that Frank was at a loss to understand. Parting his thick lips, he muttered: 'You won't be takin' me anywhere, Corrie.'

Frank was at a complete loss to understand the other's change of heart, his suddenly acquired confidence. When he did understand and half-turned at the faint movement behind him, it was already too late. He had been watching the wrong man, had his back turned to the real enemy here. He felt the impact of the heavy Colt smashing down on the side of his head as his sharp instinctive movement deflected the full force of the blow slightly. Savagely, he dragged at the butt of the Colt at his waist as Ned, coming up behind him, swung his clubbed gun for the second time, making no mistake with this blow. The heavy metal connected soggily with the back of his skull, blinding lights flared for a brief fraction of a second before his eyes, then Frank slid inertly to the ground, the half-drawn Colt sliding back into leather.

Scarcely had he hit the ground than Crenton stepped forward, reached down for his own rifle, bringing it up to cover the sprawled unconscious form, his finger tightening on the trigger. There was a snarling, bestial grimace on his face, lips thinned back over slightly parted teeth.

'This is where you get it, Corrie,' he said heavily, breathing harshly. 'No man gets the drop on me and gets away with it.'

His knuckles stood out white with

the intense pressure he was exerting. It needed only a second for him to send a slug smashing into Frank's spine. Then, sharply, from the bushes near at hand, an authoritative voice called:

'Lower that gun, Crenton. This is still a matter for the law, and while you ride with my posse you take your orders from me.' Duprey stepped into the open trail, his Colt levelled on the other.

Savagely, Crenton lowered the gun, swung away. 'What the hell does it matter, Duprey? He killed Fernandez and sure as fate he's goin' to jerk on the end of a rope. Why waste time with him? This is as good a place as any to finish it all.'

'We take him back to town for a fair trial,' snapped the sheriff. 'I warned you and Corday before, I won't have anyone takin' the law into their own hands while I'm sheriff of Fresno City.'

From a few feet away, Corday said softly: 'That is a situation that can soon be altered, Duprey.' His tone was like the hiss of a rattler. 'I daresay that Klagge won't like this when he hears of it, and since he pulls in the most votes when election of a sheriff comes around, your stay in that post may not be for quite as long as you think.'

'That may well be so,' countered Duprey. 'But so long as I am the law, things will be done exactly as I say, Klagge or not. At the moment he doesn't run the law in town. When he does, I've no doubt there will be changes made, but until then you do as I say. Now pick him up and put him into the wagon.'

He turned to the oldster standing nearby with the reversed Colt still held in his right hand. 'You all right, Jeb?'

'Sure thing, Sheriff.'

'Where's the real Ned Dryer?'

'Left him back along the trail a piece,' said Jeb. 'Had to knock him cold like this *hombre*, but I guess he'll come round in a few hours with nothin' more than a sore head to remind him of what happened.'

'How do we know he won't come round pretty soon and get back to Michener before we get into town?' demanded Crenton.

'Use sense,' said Duprey sharply. 'Without any mount, it'll take him the best part of the day to get back to the ranch, even if he does soon come round. Now let's move out. Once this *hombre* is in the town jail, I'll defy anyone to get him out until we've had the trial.'

He turned towards the trees to where two men were leading out their horses from the underbrush. He did not see the look which passed between the lawyer and Crenton; otherwise he may not have been so confident of his ability to protect Frank Corrie in the town jail.

4

Rope Justice

Frank sat on the edge of the hard bunk, his head in his hands, and tried to think clearly through the splitting ache inside his skull, staring almost without sight at the dark, hard-packed earth of the cell floor. At first, when he had come round, it had been difficult for him to orientate himself. The jolting, swaying motion under him was something he could not quite place. Then events had come back to him. He recalled his own stupidity in trusting the man with him. He had accepted the old man's story about himself in full faith and it had been this which had proved to be his undoing.

All the way into town his mind had been numbed; partly by his inability to believe that this was actually happening to him, and partly from the savage force of the blows which had knocked him unconscious. The journey back into town had taken the best part of three hours; hours torn out of nightmare as far as he had been concerned. Every jolt of the wagon had sent pain lancing fiercely through his head and body. In addition to this, the glare of the sun forced its way into his brain, even shining redly through closed lids, and the heat had been intolerable.

Some of the riders must have ridden ahead of them into town, for there had been a small crowd gathered outside the jail when they had arrived, watching as Frank was hauled unceremoniously out of the wagon and thrust up the wooden steps into the jail. He had heard the vague muttering among the men there but it was only now, since there had been a little time in which he had been able to think things out clearly, that the full significance of that rumbling mutter penetrated his numbed mind. He had temporarily forgotten the crime of which he had been falsely accused. No doubt, in spite of his lowly position, Fernandez had been well thought of in town and people would not take submissively to having his supposed murderer in the jail and not do something about it, especially if there happened to be men around ready to feed them whiskey and stir them up a little in the saloons.

Duprey had come along to the cell about half an hour earlier and recited the charge against him, had asked him if there was anything he wanted to say. Frank had known that it would be no use to protest his innocence. Everything seemed to be stacked against him; this was one of the sweetest frames he had ever come up against, and he had said nothing. After a few moments the sheriff had gone, locking the heavy door behind him, his footsteps fading along the passage. The hollow clang of the door at the far end shutting had sounded like a death knell to Frank, seated in the small cell.

At first the entire thing had seemed so strangely unreal that it was almost as if some other man was sitting there and he was watching like an outsider. But now that he was able to take everything in, calmly and coldly, assessing all of the evidence they had dispassionately, it was easy for him to see the damning build-up of the case they had against him. He rose heavily from his bunk, felt in his shirt pockets, found they had left him his tobacco and everything for the making of a smoke, twisting a quirly, lighting it, staring about him in the yellow flare of the match. It was getting dark outside now and the cell was dim.

Drawing the smoke gratefully into his lungs, he went over to the iron-grille door, pressing his face hard against the cold metal and staring as far as he could along the passage. He could just see the narrow strip of yellow under the door in the distance and he was able to pick out the faint murmur of voices as Duprey gave orders to the deputy on night duty. The sheriff's slow, measured tones came dully through the closed door, each word like a dulling vibration that jarred strangely on his eardrums. No doubt Duprey was a good sheriff, slow and methodical, honest and without too much imagination, thorough to the point of being fussy and deeply conscious of the full significance of his office. But once he stepped out of line with the plans that Klagge had for this part of the territory, he would soon cease to be sheriff. He would be replaced by a man more amenable to taking orders from the big man. Dragging the last of the smoke from the cigarette, Frank ground it out under his heel and went back to the bunk, stretching himself out on it, hands clasped behind his head, staring up at tiny small square of the grilled window set in the thick wall. Now it made a patch of deep purple where he could make out the sky through it and there were two stars just visible against the dark velvet background.

In his room at the hotel where he put up whenever he was in town on business, Austen Klagge paced back and forth, seething with a dark and furious anger, hands clasped tightly behind his back. Near the window, Laredo Ford was hunkered down, watching the rancher through half-narrowed eyes.

'If I'd asked you to make a mess of all that was to happen, you couldn't have obeyed my orders better if you'd tried.'

Corday's face was set in a sulky surliness. 'What the hell did you want us to do? Shoot Corrie down there and then with Duprey looking on? He'd have probably arrested both of us and tossed us into jail. Besides, the fewer people in town who know I'm working with you, the better, and they'd sure have guessed it if I'd shot Corrie in cold blood.'

'You know,' said Ford softly, 'I can go

over to the jail and have Corrie out in minutes. There's only a night deputy around right now. Duprey is so goddamn sure that nothin' is goin' to break, he'll have gone off for a good night's sleep. He's been in the saddle all day.'

Klagge paused in his pacing, lifted his head. 'Not an easy thing to do. He's just across the street from the jail. A warning shot from that deputy will bring him, and half the town, running. I'm not sure the time is right, either.'

Ford shrugged. 'Just a suggestion, that's all. Don't forget, though, that he's a dangerous one, that Corrie. Seems to me I've heard of him from some place back east. What I've heard, if he's the same man, I don't like. He's wizard fast with a gun and about as cute as a wide-awake rattler.'

'I know that. But this has to be done with due regard to proper legal procedure.'

'How can that possibly be done?' asked Corday, jerking his head up. His lips were pressed together in a thin line.

'It ain't so impossible.' Klagge spoke slowly. 'It'll be three or four weeks before the circuit judge gets around here. In all of that time we've got to feed this killer and that costs money. Money the town has to find.'

'So?'

'So we form a Citizens' Court, try him ourselves and carry out the sentence. If Duprey tries to interfere with the workings of such a court, he'll find he's no longer sheriff. We elected him, we can get rid of him.'

'You'll need more in on this than just yourself,' said Corday thoughtfully. 'In fact, you'll need the mayor and a handful of other influential men. Reckon you can swing them to your way of thinking?'

'I think they can be persuaded where their duty lies. We all liked Fernandez and it'll show that this town doesn't delegate its authority or shirk its duty and condone murder.'

Fent Corday remained silent, deep in

thought. Here was a decision which could affect a lot of things in town, one which made him hesitate. Not because of any feeling of squeamishness, that just was not part of his nature, and he cared little whether this man Corrie was innocent or guilty of the murder. But he could see, more clearly perhaps than any of the others in the room, that this sort of thing could quite easily backfire. It was like tipping a small boulder off the top of a cliff, watching it roll down, gathering momentum and maybe starting a regular avalanche on the way. Once things began rolling like that there was no way of telling where it would stop. Yet he also knew that in this particular deal which faced them, the stakes were much too high for him to shrink from this. He grew aware that Klagge was eyeing him closely.

'Get the mayor and some of the others over here right away, Corday,' he said sharply. 'I don't care what you have to tell them to get them here, but hurry.'

Corday got to his feet and moved to the door. 'Just one thing, Austen,' he said quietly, pausing in the doorway. 'Be sure you can control this thing once you start it.'

★ ★ ★

Consciousness was ushered in by a persistent throbbing in his head; a painful splitting ache that became more intense and agonizing the more his blurred senses cleared. Ned Dryer was lying on his back, and as he twisted his body he felt himself going over an edge and failing several feet to land with a bone-jarring thump on hard ground. Sharp-edged stones thrust themselves painfully into his flesh, even through the thick clothing he wore. He blinked open his eyes then to glaring daylight. He struggled up to a sitting position, forced himself to breathe more slowly and evenly, even though it brought on a sickening, dizzy spell that lasted for several minutes. The sunlight, glinting off the nearby rocks that loomed high over him, brought a fresh rush of pain to the front of his head, surging at the back of his temples. Reaching up, he felt the lump on the back of his head, wincing as his fingers gently explored the wound. He rose slowly on legs that seemed scarcely able to bear his weight, knees wobbling under him.

The strain and effort all added up to sheer physical exhaustion. Bitterly he could only reflect on what had happened. Judging from the position of the sun, he had been out for quite a while, two or three hours at the very least. His throat was parched and, through the sodden thickness of his thoughts, he recalled that he had passed a small waterhole just a few minutes before he had been jumped and hit on the head without warning. He moved back along the trail, seeking the spot now, but it took him the best part of fifteen minutes in his weakened state before he came upon it and sank down on to his hands and knees beside it, thrusting his face right into the water, almost falling half his length into it. It was hot, brackish, and with a sharp odour and taste, but it brought a little of the life and strength back into his body. He crawled over into the shade of a high crater of rocks, lay there for some time until the pain in his head had subsided to a dull ache. Then he went back to the water, washed some of the caked blood off the back of his head, drank his fill and got to his feet, starting on the long trek back to the Lazy T ranch.

By now the sun was dropping from the zenith but the heat still lay heavy and oppressive in the still air, with not even a breeze to bring any relief from it. All through the remaining hot, slow hours of daylight, he trudged on. At times he was scarcely aware of where he was, nor why he was doing this. All he wanted to do was lie down, close his eyes and surrender himself to the terrible weakness that lay in his limbs. But at the forefront of his mind was the inescapable knowledge that Klagge's men must have been at the back of the attack on the wagon, and the sooner he got word to Michener, the better.

It was the quiet time of the evening when he finally stumbled into the dusty courtyard facing the ranch house, more dead than alive, his feet blistered, his head a throbbing mass of pain. He half fell as he heard the shout from the direction of the bunkhouse, managed by sheer will power to hold himself upright as men came running forward, grabbing at his arms.

'Get him into the house,' said Kent Michener urgently. 'Stella, get some water boiled. We may need it. Can't say how bad he is yet.'

They half carried Ned into the parlour and laid him down on the long couch. Gently, Michener examined the contusion on the back of Dryer's head. then said heavily: 'Not as bad as I figured, but bad enough. He's been hit hard with a gunbutt, I'd say.'

'Looks to me as if he's walked for miles,' Denver opined.

On the couch, Dryer struggled to get into a sitting position, but Michener placed the flat of his hand on his chest and eased him down. 'Lie still, Ned. You've had a nasty blow on the head. You can talk in a little while.'

'Got to talk now,' Dryer mumbled. His lips were parched and cracked. Dust had worked its way into the cracks so that they hurt abominably. 'Important you know.'

'All right, Ned, I'm listening.' While Stella bathed the other's head, Michener stood at the foot of the couch, looking down at Ned. 'But take your time.'

'It was Klagge's men,' said the other slowly, hesitatingly. His thoughts were still a trifle confused. 'They jumped the wagon, knocked me cold. But I didn't lose consciousness right away. I heard 'em talkin'.'

'What were they saying?'

'Somethin' about a *hombre* called Corrie. I heard one of 'em say that this was the trail he'd be takin' and they'd be ready for him when he did show up.'

Michener held his silence for a matter of minutes or better, and at last said: 'They must've seen him leave this mornin'. Guess I wasn't as clever as I thought.'

'You think that Duprey may already have got Corrie?' asked Stella. Her tone was oddly flat and emotionless.

'It's possible. There would be too many of them for him to have much chance of taking them all.'

'Then he's in deadly danger. Once they get him into town he'll hang. Austen Klagge will see to that in spite of anything that the sheriff can do. He's only a pawn in this power game, anyway.'

'We've got no proof that they have got him,' her father said solemnly.

'Do we need proof before we go to find out?' she asked, hotly.

Michener studied the question and he tried to answer it, but he could not. He clenched and unclenched his fists helplessly. 'What do you want me to do?

Ride into town, see if they have him locked away in jail and break him out?'

'You said yourself that without a man like him we're finished. Well, we had a man and he had agreed to help us fight Klagge and everything he stood for. Now when he may need our help you're willing to stay here and let him die.'

'It's far too risky for me to ride into town. This could be just what Klagge is wanting me to do.' He shook his head slowly, emphatically. 'Much as I would like to, I can't take that chance. But I will send a man out to the line camp near the southern boundary to check on whether he got there.'

* * *

The meeting of the Citizens Committee was held in the main room of the saloon shortly before eleven o'clock that night. Klagge had realized, from the very beginning, that he had to play his cards very carefully here, in spite of the fact that he was, almost certainly, the most powerful and influential man in the territory. He had been forming his speech in his mind several minutes before the first of the men had arrived. Ed Tannadyce, the recently elected mayor, was a fat, balding man, perspiring profusely as he came in, in spite of the fact that the night air was cool now. He threaded his way among the card tables to where Klagge stood against the bar, flanked by Ford and Rand.

Mopping his forehead with a large red handkerchief, he said gaspingly: 'What is all this about, Klagge? If it's town business, surely it can wait until the morning.'

'Now, now, Ed, calm yourself. We just have to discuss a point of law and I need your help. After all, as mayor of the town, you have not only the right but the duty to be here.'

'Very well.' Tannadyce sank down into a chair at the nearby table. 'I suppose you've got your reasons for this, though I'm damned if I can see the urgency.'

'You will in a little while.' Klagge turned back to the bar and poured himself another drink. He had already decided how he would go about this. He prided himself on being an excellent judge of human nature. With these people, all he would have to do would be to make them conscious of their own importance, put the thought of action into their minds so that it would appear that they, and not him, had made the decision to try and hang Corrie. That way, there would be no repercussions as far as he was concerned when it was all over; and if Duprey tried to interfere and stand on his rights as sheriff, it would be a relatively simple matter to depose him.

At this moment he felt certain that the sheriff would be the only man against what he intended to do. During the next five minutes the rest of the committee came in. Sam Vickers, the banker, fussy and pompous, but shrewd in spite of his outward appearance; Forbes Warren, the landowner, who held the deeds to most of the land on which the town had been built; Cy Hewitt, owner of the Silver Lode mine and lastly, Fent Corday.

There were also several of his own men lounging against the bar or along the walls of the room. With them there, the Citizens Committee would be just a little more anxious to listen to what he had to say. He knew all of these men intimately, but there were one or two of them, Hewitt in particular, one could never really get to know in a hundred years. It was impossible to guess what went on in his head.

Clearing his throat, he moved away from the bar and stood facing them. Boots and chairs scraped noisily as they settled back and waited for him to speak. He noticed Hewitt eyeing him with a vaguely wondering look, evidently puzzled.

'Gentlemen,' he began, speaking quite casually and naturally, 'I've asked you all to come here tonight because something important has come up and I feel it's essential that we should get it cleared up right now rather than let things drag along, as they will if we don't take immediate action.'

'What sort of things are you talkin' about, Austen?' asked Hewitt.

'I'm talking about this killer the sheriff brought in this afternoon. The man who shot down Fernandez in cold blood yesterday morning.'

Hewitt kept his eyes fixed on Klagge, but he did not nod his head, or make any movement at all. Klagge thought: he's not going to be an easy one to convince. We may have to go through with this without him.

'The way I figure it, this town is big enough now to be able to take care of its own affairs. We don't have to wait for Judge Fenton to take his time getting here to try every murderer we bring in. I say that we have both the right and the need to try these killers ourselves, and if we find 'em guilty, then we carry out the sentence right here in town. What's going to happen as far as Corrie is concerned? He stays in jail, gets three meals a day, all paid for by the citizens of the town. Then he gets his trial and, when he's found guilty, he has to be taken back to Fort Arthur to be hung there.' He paused significantly. 'Ain't no guarantee either that he'll ever get there. Plenty of men have escaped from custody in the past and they're still roamin' the territory, ready to kill again. But if we go through with it, we'll be goddamn certain he won't kill any more innocent men.'

'Mister Klagge has got a point there,' spoke up Corday from the back of the room. 'We can appoint defending and prosecuting counsels from among us, see he gets a fair trial, and then carry out the sentence.'

'Hold up a minute,' said Hewitt. 'Seems to me you're all jumping into this with one idea in your minds. You've all made up your minds that he's guilty. What sort of trial is he going to get if you think that?'

Klagge cleared his throat again, swore at Hewitt in his mind. He might have known the other would prove to be a stumbling block. It would have been better if they had gone ahead without him. He said, almost angrily now: 'You've got it all wrong, Cy. Sure, all of the evidence points to his guilt. After all, he was seen spurrin' away from the livery stables just after the shot had been fired, moments before the body was discovered. We know he went there to buy a horse. We've got his own admission of that, as well as the fact that he's riding the black bay. But he'll get a fair hearing. If you're so certain he's innocent, then we'll appoint you as his defending counsel.'

Hewitt half turned in his chair to stare at the others. Then he turned back and lapsed into silence.

'I think you see my point,' went on Klagge smugly. 'Why should killers be allowed to sit there in the jail, maybe while somebody in the territory is scheming to get them out. We all know where he was found. Working for Kent Michener.' Klagge was not sure whether he had done the right thing mentioning this. Everyone in Fresno City knew the antagonism which existed between Michener and himself, and it was possible they might put a different construction on to his determination to try Corrie here and now, instead of waiting for the due processes of the law to take their normal course.

'Surely you don't think that Michener will ride into town and try to break him out of jail, do you?' asked Tannadyce.

'Why not? He's always said that he means to bring gunhawks into the territory to fight me. This *hombre* is one of them. He's the first. But if we weaken and back down now, then he won't be the last. Before we know where we are, Michener will have brought in an army of hired killers and we'll be in the middle of a full-scale range war.'

He noticed, with a feeling of satisfaction, the expression of alarm that flitted swiftly over the other's flabby features. Evidently even the threat of such a happening was enough to scare the mayor. Pressing his point home, he went on quickly: 'But if we act firmly and decisively now, it will stop Michener from going ahead with any such plans he may have.'

'I agree with Austen,' said Corday quietly. 'We simply cannot afford to be complacent about this. Indecision will be fatal. After all, we have to think of everyone living in the town. We're the committee and it's up to us to see that their lives are protected from killers such as Corrie, and that their money isn't wasted keeping a murderer alive any longer than is absolutely necessary.'

'But what will Duprey say to this?' inquired Warren, sitting forward in his chair. 'He won't like it if we go over there and drag Corrie out of the jail.'

'If he doesn't like it, then he knows what he can do,' Klagge said harshly.

'We elected him to that post and he's answerable to us. Why should we wait on the convenience of the law nearly ninety miles away? We have our own brand of law here in Fresno City and it's good enough for us. Anyone here who doesn't want to be in with us can just get up and leave right now. If there is nobody, then we can nominate the officials.'

He looked directly at Hewitt as he spoke, watching the man's face for any sign of emotion. For several seconds the mine owner seemed to be struggling with his conscience. Then he said harshly: 'I know that I ought to get up and walk right out of here, Klagge. I don't agree with what you're trying to do. The law has already been established here, even though we are a frontier town and ninety miles from the County seat — and Duprey is the official representative. But I figure that someone has to stick around to see that this doesn't turn into the sort of lynching party some of you want, in spite of the high-sounding words and phrases that have been used to dress it up. So I'll accept that offer of defending counsel.'

'Then we'll get on with it.' Klagge looked at each of the others in turn. This was the only way to do it, push everything through fast so that they had no time to really consider things, and it would be over before they got around to asking themselves why they were doing it and whether it was right or not.

* * *

The thunderous knocking on the street door roused the deputy from his doze. For a moment, jerking upright in his chair, he stared about him in the dimness, then slowly lowered his feet from the top of the desk, fastened on his gunbelt and walked to the door, wondering who could be hammering there at that time of night. He risked a quick look through the window near the door, felt both surprise and a tinge of fear as he noticed the group of men standing outside. For a second, he debated whether to leave the door locked and bolted, grab a rifle off the wall and trust that he would be able to hold out until the sound brought Duprey running. He was unsure of himself of what he should do in these circumstances.

The knocking ceased for a moment and then he heard Mayor Tannadyce's voice call loudly: 'Open this door. We've got business with your prisoner.'

The deputy hesitated for a moment, then told himself that it would surely be all right to open for the Mayor. Tannadyce was the last person in town who would be associated with anything outside of the law.

Unlocking the door, he unbolted it and then stood on one side as the men came in. His eyes were on the men in front, but he was conscious of Austen Klagge moving in behind the rest and Fent Corday, the shifty-eyed lawyer, who he neither liked nor trusted. 'What do you want?' he asked tightly.

'We've come for Corrie,' said Klagge harshly.

'What for?' For the first time, the deputy now felt sure he had done the wrong thing in opening the door. He wondered whether to run and fetch Duprey, feeling certain this was a lynching party in spite of Tannadyce's presence among them.

'We aim to give him his trial a little earlier than he expects,' Klagge said, pushing him roughly out of the way. 'Now get those keys of yours and bring him out here.'

'But you can't do that,' protested the other. 'I've got to have Sheriff Durey's say-so before I can let him out.'

'You've got our say-so,' hissed Klagge. 'Now hurry along there and do as you're told. This is the Citizens' Committee, and we aim to see that no more of the town's money is wasted on the likes of him.'

The deputy turned apealingly to the mayor. Tannadyce wiped his face, nodded. 'Better do as he says, George. We don't want any more trouble here.'

'But the Sheriff — '

'We'll take care of Duprey, all in good time,' put in Corday. 'This is all legal and above board. Hewitt here is the defending counsel, and the mayor has been nominated judge. It won't take long, then you can get some sleep.'

'I take orders from Sheriff Duprey, Mayor. Not from you or any of the committee you've brought along with you.'

Tannadyce hesitated and, from the rear, Klagge saw the hesitation, knew that he had to do something or the rest of the men might decide they didn't want to go through with this. Harshly, he said: 'Laredo! Think you can make this man have a little more respect for the senior citizens of this town?'

'Sure, Mister Klagge.' Laredo pushed forward through the small crowd of men near the doorway, a faint grin on his face. He walked right up to the deputy. The man stood his ground, his fingers resting on the gunbutt in his belt. He was scared but trying hard not to show it, believing himself to be in the right, wishing that Duprey was there.

Laredo stood with his feet slightly apart, his hands hanging loosely by his sides, his leering face thrust forward into the other's. Then, without warning, his right hand tightened into a fist and he swung hard, driving a blow at the deputy's face, sending him hurtling backward against the edge of the desk. The sharp strip of wood caught the other hard in the kidneys, wrenching a cry of agony from his bleeding lips. He caught himself before going down and hung there, his head wobbling on his shoulders, the blood dripping slowly from his smashed mouth.

'He says he's willin' to do as you say now, Mister Klagge,' said Laredo. The vicious, animal-like grin was still etched on his face.

'Good.'

Weakly, the deputy pulled himself upright, shaking his head to clear it. He went behind the desk, picked up the bunch of keys and opened the door on the far side of the room. Three minutes later he was back with Frank Corrie.

Blinking against the yellow glare from the lantern on the desk, Frank stared at the ring of men facing him. He recognized some of them, wondered what was coming next.

'What is this?' he said harshly. 'A lynchin' party? Reckon it's just the sort of justice I'd expected in this town.'

'You'll find out what it is soon enough,' retorted Klagge. He nodded to Laredo. 'Bring him over to the saloon. We'll sew this thing up fast.'

'A kangaroo court.' Frank smiled contemptuously. 'I figured as much. Just an attempt to whitewash yourselves. Why don't you come right out with it?'

'Shut up!' snarled Klagge. 'Now get over the street to the saloon.'

The deputy, nursing his torn mouth, waited until the crowd had moved over the street, then ran as fast as his shaking

143

legs would carry him for Duprey. The sheriff had heard some of the commotion and was on his way at a quick pace along the street when the deputy caught him.

'What's goin' on back there, George?' he demanded roughly.

'It's Klagge. They've formed a Citizens' Committee. Came for the prisoner, took him across to the saloon. 'They aim to try him there tonight.'

'They can't do that,' muttered Duprey. He hitched his gunbelt a little higher about his waist, and fell into step beside the deputy.

By the time they reached the saloon the trial had already begun. Frank Corrie was seated in a chair in front of the bar and there were some of Klagge's boys ranged around the walls, ready for any sign of trouble.

Pushing the doors open with the flat of his hands, Duprey went inside. He felt the air of heightened tension in the saloon the moment he stepped in.

Klagge was speaking from near the

bar. 'The charge against the prisoner is that he deliberately shot down Fernandez in cold blood before taking the bay and ridin' out of town. Right now I'm going to establish the truth of this. Then the prisoner will have his say, and after that we'll vote on whether or not he's guilty.'

'You're talkin' mighty big, Klagge.' Duprey strode forward. 'Who gave you the right to usurp the law?'

Klagge swung on him sharply. His eyes narrowed down a little and his lips grew tight He paused for a moment, then said tersely: 'We've already been into this, Clem. Ain't no call for you to get yourself all steamed up. There are all the most influential and responsible citizens of Fresno City here. We've decided to try this *hombre* and, if we find him guilty, then he'll hang at dawn tomorrow.'

'You know damned well this is illegal.'

'I know nothin' of the kind. This is a big enough community to be able to decide its own destiny. We don't intend waiting for the circuit judge to put in an appearance before he's tried. All of the witnesses are here and we mean to get on with it without any interference from anyone.'

'You'll damned well get interference from me,' Duprey said sharply. 'I'm the law's representative here and that man is my prisoner. My orders are to hold any prisoners until the judge gets around to holding court. You can't just up and take the law into your own hands just because you figure it's more convenient.'

'We're doing it,' said Klagge flatly. 'Just remember that we were the ones who passed you as sheriff here. Now if you don't want to co-operate, just say so. I figure we can always get ourselves a new sheriff.'

Duprey stared at the other sharply. So that was the way things were lying. He might have guessed it would come to a showdown like this sooner or later. Klagge had never liked him, even when he had been voted into office. This was his chance to get rid of him and he was seizing it with both hands, reckoning that he now had the backing of all the men in the saloon.

Deliberately ignoring Klagge, Duprey turned to face Tannadyce and Vickers. He said tautly: 'You two throwin' in your lot with this killer?'

Klagge grinned mirthlessly before either of the two men could answer. 'You seem to be mighty free with your insults tonight, Duprey. But I'm not a man to hold any grudge. If you're convinced you want no part of this, then I reckon you'd be best out of office.'

'I wasn't directin' my remarks your way, Klagge. I'm talking to the mayor and Mister Vickers. You want to go through with this illegal act?'

Tannadyce spoke up slowly. 'The way we see it, Duprey, Klagge is right. It's only logical that we should take care of our own town rather than have to delegate our authority to Fort Arthur, ninety miles away. They're completely out of touch with events here in Fresno City.'

'I see.' Bitterness edged Duprey's voice. He felt the dull wash of anger in his mind. Impulsively he tore the star off his shirt, tossed it on to the floor at Tannadyce's feet. 'Then I reckon you'd better find another man for this job. If I had to go through with it another day, it'd stick in my craw. You're no better than Klagge and his band of hired gunslingers. You don't want law and order, you just want to think that you're almighty, important members of the community. This is lynch law, mob rule, whichever way you care to look at it.'

He spun sharply on his heel, and made for the door with the deputy trailing along behind him. He was halfway there when Klagge called suddenly: 'Just where do you figure you're going, Duprey?'

'I'm gettin' out of this place. Suddenly the air in here stinks in my nostrils. Maybe I'll let the rest of the town know what's going on in the saloon. Could be there are a few decent citizens still left in Fresno City.'

'Not so fast. You're not going any place. If you reckon you can move around town and stir up trouble for us, you're wrong.'

'You goin to try to stop me, Klagge?' said Duprey dangerously. He turned to face the rancher, his hands hanging loosely at his side, fingers spread out rigidly just above the butts of the Colts at his waist, spread like the spokes of a wheel. His gaze locked with the other's.

'Maybe he won't right now, but I will,' said Ford. He was no longer lounging, apparently unconcerned, against the wall, but had pushed himself away from it, the sixgun in his right hand levelled on Duprey's chest. There was a loud click, an explosive sound in the unnatural stillness of the saloon as he thumbed back the hammer.

Duprey let his hands fall away from his guns. To try to go for them would have been worse than useless, but for just a second the thought of action had lived in his mind.

'That's better,' said Klagge. 'Now both of you men unbuckle your gunbelts and sit down. This won't take long and then we can decide what to do with you.'

Corday, seated at one of the tables, said with a derisive laugh: 'I guess we might even charge 'em with obstructing the process of the law, Austen.'

There was a gust of laughter from the other men in the saloon. Ford came forward and kicked the fallen gunbelts into one corner, then went back to his original position against the wall, watching the proceedings with flat, seemingly uninterested eyes.

'Right,' said Klagge, instantly brisk now that the danger from Duprey was past. He felt more relieved about it than he showed to the others. He had, in fact, anticipated a lot more trouble. He was glad things had been resolved as quickly and as easily as this. Now to get to the point quick.

'All right, since I'm the prosecuting counsel, I'll give you all the facts. Two days ago this *hombre* arrived in town on the stage. He put up at the hotel for the night and, at first light the next morning, he went along to the livery stables, after inquiring at the hotel and in the restaurant where he could buy himself a good horse. Nobody knows what really happened in the stables that morning, but one shot was fired and, a few moments later, as Fent Corday will testify, he was seen riding hell for leather away from the stables on the black bay. By the time anybody got to the stables, Fernandez was dead. The sheriff, whether he likes to testify or not, was one of the first there, and there was no sign of anyone else. It was still too early for most of the townsfolk to be up and about. Now I'm putting it to the jury that there was only one man who could've shot Fernandez down in cold blood and that man is Frank Corrie.' He pointed an accusing finger in

Frank's direction.

'Then you're a goddamn liar.' Frank jumped to his feet, facing the other. 'Fernandez was alive when I left him and, as for the bay, I paid the price he asked for that horse.'

'Sit down,' shouted Klagge. 'You'll get your chance to speak later.'

'Some chance that's goin' to be with a rigged jury here,' Frank said thinly.

'Silence!' said Tannadyce in a voice that startled even himself. 'You can't help your case, young fellow, by making these wild accusations. Do you agree with what Austen Klagge has said, Fent? Did you witness this man leaving the stables shortly after the shot was fired?'

'That's the truth, Mayor.' Corday rose to his feet. 'I'd just stepped out of my office when the shot sounded along the street. Less than half a minute later this man rode out on the black bay and headed out of town.'

'You're certain it was after the shot and not before?'

'I'm positive about that.' The lawyer nodded his head emphatically. 'It was the sound of the shot that made me look up.'

'Then I reckon we've established that fact,' Klagge murmured smugly. 'And Fernandez was dead when you reached him.'

'Shot from close range. There were powder burns on his shirt front.'

'I see. Thank you. As you see, we now know that Corrie was there when this man was murdered and he lit out of town within moments of the fatal shot. Seems there's nothing much more for me to say, except that there's no doubt in my mind as to his guilt.' He sat down, gave a brief nod towards Hewitt.

The mine owner got to his feet. He seemed a little uncomfortable as he faced the others. 'I only took this job because it seemed to me that nobody else was going to volunteer to defend this man. You'd all made up your minds that he was guilty and it wasn't going to be any sort of trial at all.'

'Get on with what you have to say,' interrupted Klagge. 'It's past midnight and we don't want to be here all night debating legal arguments.'

Hewitt swung on him. 'Like I said, you all believe he's guilty. You, Klagge, because you want him dead. Somebody else here because he's probably the real killer and, as for the rest of you, all you do is follow Klagge's lead like sheep without minds of your own. But to get to the point. Nobody saw this man fire that shot, so there's not a shred of real evidence that he did. We've only got Corday's word for it that he didn't leave before the shot. And what's just as important, nobody has provided him with any motive for wanting to kill Fernandez. Seems the money he paid for the bay was still in the groom's pocket when he was found, so he didn't do it to steal the horse. Klagge and Corday have talked a lot about him probably knowing Fernandez from some time in the past, that this was a vengeance killing. Here again there's no proof of that. So what are we left with? A man arrives in town, kills a groom for no reason at all and then rides on out. But he doesn't keep on riding. He hires up with one of the ranchers in the territory, whereas if he really was the killer, then he'd keep moving on as fast as he could once his chore was finished.'

'It's happened before,' said Klagge. 'Some critters don't need a reason to kill. It's in their blood.'

Hewitt was controlled and he still made an effort, even though he knew it would do no good. These men were in a neck-stretching mood and nothing he could do or say was going to shake them. Until they had taken over Sheriff Duprey, he thought there might have been a chance, but not now. 'You've still got no evidence at all, Klagge, that he had anything to do with Fernandez's murder.'

'We'll let the members of the jury decide that,' Klagge said confidently. 'I figure they can put the facts together.'

The group of men seated at one of the tables conferred together for a few moments, then Warren got heavily to his feet, nodded slowly. 'Takin' all of the facts into consideration,' he said gravely. 'We've reached the conclusion that the prisoner is guilty of shootin' Fernandez in cold blood.'

Klagge nodded in satisfaction as he leaned against the bar. He threw a quick sideways glance in Tannadyce's direction, wondered whether the old fool would be able to go through with his part now. The mayor caught his look, interpreted its meaning correctly and got slowly to his feet, gripping the edge of the table with his fingers. There was a thin sheen of sweat on his florid features and for a moment he fumbled in his pocket for his handkerchief, then decided that to mop his face now would be a sign of weakness in front of every man in the saloon. Drawing himself up to his full height, he said in a hoarse tone: 'I find myself in complete agreement with the verdict which has been reached. There is only one sentence for such a crime. Frank Corrie is hereby sentenced to hang for the shooting of Fernandez.'

'When is the sentence to be carried out?' Klagge prompted as the other made to resume his seat.

'At dawn tomorrow.' Tannadyce looked as if he wished he were a thousand miles away from there at that moment. But he had got it out. He had done as Klagge had said. Now he wanted to wash his hands of the whole sordid affair.

Klagge grinned triumphantly. He nodded towards two of his men. 'Take Corrie back across to the jail, put him in the cell again. I reckon he'll be safe enough there until we come for him in the morning, and he'll have all of the night to reflect on the error of his ways.'

'What do we do with Duprey and the deputy?' said Fent Corday.

'Lock them up for the night too. They may try to stir up things in town if we left them alone.'

'Could be we could hang 'em too,' murmured Ford softly.

Klagge hesitated and then shook his head. The thought had occurred to him, but he had reluctantly dismissed it. There would be hell to pay if they hanged two lawmen here. Far better to run them out of town once Corrie was dead.

5

Gunman's Bluff

Frank did not sleep at all that night after they had dragged him back to the cell in the town jail. He was only too acutely aware of the danger of his position for any rest to be possible. He knew that Duprey and his deputy had been locked up in one of the other cells and there would be no help for him from that quarter.

Outside, through the window, he could hear some sounds of activity in the town, guessed that some of the citizens were already up and about. There was a faint silver gleam just visible, indicating that the dawn was almost at hand.

Duprey's voice reached him from along the narrow passage. 'You awake, Corrie?'

'Sure. You think I could sleep?' There was a note of irony in his voice.

'I just want you to know that after what happened in the saloon last night, I'm convinced you didn't kill Fernandez. I know it makes little difference now what I think, but I figured you'd like to know.'

'Thanks.'

'I don't feel very good about this, Corrie. Maybe I should've taken more men with me last night, but I never figured the others would join in with Klagge.'

'I reckon some of them don't think when they have a man like that talkin' to them,' Frank said tightly. 'He didn't have much trouble in building up a damning case against me. What do you figure they'll do with you?'

'You heard what was said. They'll get another man for sheriff. Somebody who'll do just as Klagge orders. As for George and me, maybe they'll give us an hour to get out of town with the threat of shootin' us down if we show our faces here again.'

'I wonder what Michener is doin' right now?' said the deputy. 'Reckon he must know what's happened if Ned Dryer has got back to the Lazy T ranch. Could be he'll ride into town to find out what happened to you.'

'Even if he did, do you reckon he could do anything? When they take me out there, Klagge will have plenty of his men scattered around in the crowd, ready for any trouble. He knows he's got to go through with this before he can move against Michener.'

There was the creak of the passage door opening. A moment later heavy footsteps sounded. Laredo and Jose came along the corridor, stopped outside Frank's cell. Laredo grinned, his teeth white in the shadow of his face. 'This is it, killer,' he said viciously. He turned the key effortlessly in the lock, swung open the door and stepped inside while his companion stood outside with a gun trained on Frank. Twisting Corrie's arm behind him, he thrust him up on to his toes, and forced him out of the cell. The door was shut behind him and he was propelled along into the outer office where Klagge and several of the other men were waiting.

'You're sure that Duprey and the other man are safely under lock and key so they can't butt in on the proceedings?' Klagge said.

Laredo nodded. 'They're safe enough.'

'Good. Bring him along. We're getting everything ready in the square.'

Frank was hustled out of the jail into the street. In the grey light he saw that quite a large crowd had gathered there and felt a faint sense of surprise to notice several women among the onlookers. It was as if this was a festive occasion and nobody wanted to miss a thing.

With Laredo and Jose gripping his arms, he had no choice but to move along the street in the direction of the square. Some of the men in the crowd were moving quickly along the back of the rows of spectators, keeping pace with the small procession. Others had gone on ahead to the square, evidently knowing that the hanging was to take place there. Frank eyed them bleakly. He felt a surge of bitterness, almost amounting to anger, at the eager way in which these people were out, waiting to witness the hanging of an innocent man. He wondered how many of them really knew what was happening, or that Klagge was deliberately manipulating this for his own ends. Maybe some day they would realize that an innocent man had been hanged and that the killer was still among them.

Who could it be? he wondered. Maybe Klagge himself, or either of the two men holding his arms, acting on Klagge's orders. Maybe someone not connected with Klagge in any way. Some man nursing a private grudge against the man, shooting him down within seconds, it seemed, of him riding out on the horse he had just bought.

Now they were walking past the livery stables where it had all happened.

Frank did not turn his head to look, knowing that Klagge, walking a short distance behind, was watching him closely every step of the way. Maybe he expected to see him crack under the strain. Well, he was going to be deprived of that particular pleasure.

There was a tall cottonwood tree in the centre of the town square. It looked so large and old that it must have been there from the very beginning and the town had probably been built around it. Now it stood as a monument to what had been before the building of the town.

Two men were already at the tree, one swarming up on to the stout branch which stretched outward almost at right angles to the main trunk. A rope had been brought and was being looped over the branch, the noose at the end hanging just a little higher than a man's head if he was seated on a horse.

A man had gone into the livery stable. He returned a few moments later with a horse, leading it carefully into the square. It carried a bridle but no saddle. The man holding the end of the noose jerked it hard, pulling on it with all of his weight before he was finally satisfied.

'All right,' called Klagge. 'Mount him up. We've wasted enough time. We'll show Michener and any of the others that it won't help them to bring in killers to start any trouble in Fresno City.'

'You want me to tie his hands?' asked Faredo. He produced a short length of rope.

'Might as well,' said Klagge with a harsh laugh. 'Not that this is goin' to last long.'

'You're crazy, Klagge,' Frank said tightly through thinned lips. 'You think you've got it good now and you're ridin' high. But there'll come a time — and very soon — when you won't be the top dog here any longer, when people will start askin' questions and wantin' to know the proper answers.

Then I reckon they'll figure out for themselves who's the real murderer in this part of the territory and you'll be danglin' on the end of a rope like this.'

'String him up,' snarled Klagge viciously. He stepped back to have a better view of the proceedings.

Laredo and Jose lifted him on to the back of the horse while another man held it steady with the bridle. Laredo edged forward a little behind him, began to twine the rope around his wrists, to lash them at his back. 'You got any last-minute prayers you want to say, Corrie,' he grinned, 'reckon you'd better say 'em now. You won't get another chance.'

One of the mounted men rode his horse close alongside Frank's, reached up to grab the noose and adjust it around Frank's neck. There was a faint mutter from the crowd gathered around the square.

'Hurry it up!' called Klagge. 'Get that rope round his neck and let's have this over with. Nearly time for breakfast.'

166

Frank tensed himself as the rider leaned close. He comprehended that his time was swiftly running out and it was hard to realize that it had to end like this, a horrible, degrading death strangling on the end of a rope, accused of a crime he hadn't committed.

He wished now that he had made a fight for it at the beginning. It was too late now for him to do anything and he could expect no help from any of the crowd watching with avid anticipation.

The man was in the act of slipping the noose around his neck when the totally unexpected interruption came. It was a measure of the concentration of the crowd that none of them had seen the lone rider move along the deserted street from the north. The first any of them knew of it was when the girl's clear, ringing voice said:

'Call your dogs off, Klagge, or you'll be the first man to die!'

Klagge whirled at the words. Frank turned his head with a wrench of neck muscles. Stella Michener sat her mount easily. She seemed perfectly composed. There was nothing wrong with the way she held the shotgun either. It was pointed directly at Klagge and, from that distance, she could take more than a dozen men with him if she let loose with both barrels, and the men knew it. As they stepped away from him, Frank tore his hands free, thrust away the dangling noose and kneed the horse forward until he was clear of the men.

'Thanks,' he said, and his voice sounded strange through the buzzing in his ears. 'I never thought I'd see you here.'

'I guessed there might be something like this going on if Klagge had a hand in it,' Stella said. Her voice was hard. She did not look at him as she spoke, but kept her gaze on the crowd in front of her.

Frank paused for a moment, then he said: 'Think you can hold off these men while I get my own horse and guns? Guess I feel kinda naked without 'em.'

For the first time there was a faint

smile on the girl's lips. 'They won't make any trouble. I wasn't fool enough to ride in alone with just this shotgun. If they figure I'm bluffing, maybe they'd care to take a look at the windows yonder. There are a dozen rifles trained on them right now. The first man to make a move we don't like gets a bullet in him where it hurts.'

Frank saw the heads of the folk in the crowd turn almost as one man. Instinctively, he glanced up himself, let his gaze wander over the windows in the upper floors of the houses around the square. The first rays of the rising sun glinted on the shiny barrels of the rifles there, poking down and covering everyone in the crowd.

'You didn't miss a trick, did you?' he said, with a touch of admiration in his tone.

Wheeling his mount, he rode back around the circle of townsfolk, found his own mount in the stables and threw a saddle on him, tightening the cinch under the animal's belly before swinging up and riding out once more. Nothing had changed in the square. Under the threat of the guns, no one wanted to take any chance of being shot, but there was no telling how long the status quo would last, and Frank paused only to take the gunbelt from the sullen-faced Laredo before gigging his mount away until he was beside the girl.

'Ride on out of town,' she said sharply.

'But what about you?'

'Don't worry on my account. I can take care of myself.'

Frank was still uncertain of this, even with those men up at the windows. 'Hurry!' snapped Stella Michener, a note of urgent anger in her tone. 'These men won't stand here for ever.'

'Quit tellin' me to save my own skin,' he retorted. 'If we go, then we go together.'

The girl made to make a further sharp retort, then bit it down as she saw the look of determination on his face.

Without a word, she gave a signal to the men at the windows, sharply wheeled her mount about, kicking at its flanks with her heels. Frank turned and rode after her.

They did not speak until they were the best part of a mile out of Fresno City and Frank was certain they had not been followed. Then he reined up and let his mount pick its own pace.

'I didn't kill that Mexican groom,' he said after a brief pause. 'Do you believe that?'

'Does it really matter what I believe?' She did not turn her head to look at him as she spoke, but continued to look straight in front of her, head lifted high, shoulders straight.

'I think it does. After all, you must have had some reason for risking your life riding into town like that.'

'All right then. I don't think you did it. As I said before, you're not the usual kind of trail-jumper we get riding through these parts. There's something more to you than that, though right now I'm not sure what it is. But I don't think you would shoot a man down without giving him an even chance and, if you did, you wouldn't put your head back into a noose by riding in as you did, bringing one of the men Klagge killed back to the ranch.'

'How did you know there was somethin' wrong?'

'That wasn't hard to work out. Ned rolled into the ranch last night, more dead than alive; told us that some of Klagge's men had stopped him and taken the wagon, after knocking him out. My father sent a man out to the line camp near the creek to see if you'd found your way there, and when he came back early in the morning with the news you hadn't been seen, I guessed that Klagge and the posse must have been lying in wait for you somewhere along the trail, so I got a bunch of the boys together and we rode into town just as they dragged you out of the jail-house. They were far too interested in watching you to see what we were doing.'

'It was a nice little trap,' he acknowledged. 'But those men back there. How will they manage to get out of town? Klagge has plenty of his men there.'

'They know what they're doing. Besides, they have some old scores to settle with Klagge and his gunhawks.'

*　*　*

Anger seething away inside him, like something alive gnawing at his vitals, Austen Klagge was forced to stand by helplessly while Corrie and Stella Michener rode out of town. Moistening his lips, he gazed after them and then turned his attention on the windows above the square. To his chagrin, he saw that they were all empty. A few seconds fled before the truth penetrated. Then the anger flared up savagely.

'Get along the street and stop those Lazy T men,' he yelled at the top of his voice. 'They're tryin' to get away.'

Laredo and Jose were already running to the corner of the square, their bodies crouched low. Jose had his sixgun out and Laredo carried the Winchester from his saddle pouch. They went down on their knees behind a couple of barrels on the boardwalk and commenced firing along the street. The rest of his men rushed forward, gained the street. The quick, lean report of a rifle came from somewhere beyond the livery stables and he saw one of his men pitch forward on to his knees in the dust, lying still as he crashed face downward. More gunfire burst up with a sultry violence. Running forward, Klagge approached the entrance to the main street where it joined the square. Dust had formed a silver screen through which he was able to make out details only indistinctly. There was a loose bunch of riders halfway along the street, the horses breaking under the sudden fire of other guns.

Klagge yelled an order, jerking his own gun from its holster and loosing off a couple of wild shots which hit nothing. He could see the Lazy T men struggling to bring their horses under control, knew that if they once managed this they would be able to ride unhindered through the far side of town and there would be nothing he and his men could do to stop them since their own mounts were tethered in front of the saloon and the jail-house some fifty yards along the street nearer the riders. To attempt to get to them would be sheer suicide.

More gunfire came from the Lazy T riders and Klagge dropped full length into the dust as bullets hummed close to him. Cursing, he aimed at the lunging men, saw one of them sway back in the saddle as a bullet found its mark, but the man managed to stay upright, grasping tightly on to the reins, moving his horse further along the street as the rest of Michener's men began to follow him. He heard more of his men yell and drop as the final volley tore into them. Lead flailed at the wooden uprights along the nearby boardwalk with a terrible intensity. Wooden chips flew over his prone body and he held his breath as for long seconds the firing grew in its intensity. It all seemed to be smashing along the street where he lay and he cowered in the dust, head pulled down into his arms, not daring to lift it. Every muscle in him was pulled so tight under the flesh that it set up its own individual ache. Cramp clawed through his legs with lancing fingers of agony. But his mind was very clear and very sharp. He had somehow allowed a mere slip of a girl to pull a stunt like that and gain the upper hand over him; just as he had been about to finish Corrie. Now that man was still alive, still something to be reckoned with.

Dragging himself forward with his arms, moving his legs in great heaves, he gained the comparative sanctuary of the sidewalk, flung himself down on it, following the shift of the firing with his ears. Every sound seemed to be curiously magnified in enhanced importance.

The shouting went on as his men began to move forward, firing as they went. The gunfire seemed to be breaking out first in one spot and then another. But gradually it was fading until there was only the occasional shot, accompanied by slowly atrophying echoes. Lifting his head, he peered through the dust screen. Nothing happened and in his ears, just audible above the echoes of the gunfire, there was the steady abrasion of hoofbeats fading swiftly into the distance.

Anger and thwarted vengeance threatened to overwhelm him. Thrusting the Colt back into its holster, he stepped down into the street. Laredo came running over.

'You want us to saddle up and go after 'em?'

Klagge's eyes pinched down. The set, almost wooden, expression on his face did not alter in the slightest, but a faint edge of contempt blended with frustrated wrath crept into his tone. 'You couldn't stop them here, you won't be able to out there.'

'But goddamn! They had a dozen rifles trained on us.'

'Sure. And there were more than a score of you scattered throughout the crowd, supposed to be looking for trouble. How'd that girl get so close without being spotted?' His voice lashed the other savagely. 'Never mind. It's done now. As for going after those Lazy T riders, they'll be in the hills by now and in that dust it'll take an Apache to trail them once they hit the rocks. I want you over in the hotel. Bring Jose and Corday with you.'

Turning on his heel without a backward glance, knowing the order would be carried out at once, Klagge went over to the hotel, took his key and climbed the stairs to his room. The three men he had summoned followed less than five minutes later.

Klagge's cigar had gone out and he ran a freshening match up and down across the blunt tip of it, cheeks drawing in as he puffed on it. Snapping the match in half with a brief twist of his finger and thumb, he tossed it out of the open window.

Fent Corday lowered himself into a chair. There was a distinct air of tension crackling in the room. Corday missed none of this. Klagge had just suffered a big and ignominious defeat and somebody was going to have to bear the brunt of his wrath. The silence drew out. In the street outside a lone rider loped past.

Blowing smoke in a cloud in front of him, Klagge suddenly turned to Laredo. 'You line up those riders I asked about?'

Laredo nodded, lips twisted into a faint smile, a strange glint in his eyes.

'I got them. Ten, all of the right kind. They should start drifting in any time now.'

'The sooner, the better. I never figured this hombre Corrie would sign on for Michener. Means we could have big trouble there now if he gets any more men like that to ride for him.'

Corday stirred in his chair. 'I'm wondering if it wouldn't be a good idea to start working hard on Michener right now. That dozen men or so who held up everybody in the square a little while ago. They're probably all the good men he's got. You could rustle up three times that number quite easily, men used to handling guns. Hit him real hard before he's ready — tonight! You don't have to worry about Duprey now. Spread it around he was really in cahoots with Corrie. That should ease the consciences of the townsfolk a bit, and the fact that Lazy T men helped free that killer when we had him on the gallows after a fair trial will give you the legal excuse you need to attack Michener for aiding and harbouring a convicted murderer.'

A glint showed abruptly in Klagge's eyes. 'You've got a point there.' He grinned. 'And since the town is now short on one sheriff and a deputy, I guess it's time we put that to rights. Fent, I want you to witness that I'm now appointing these two men the law in Fresno City.'

For a moment the lawyer stared at the rancher in surprise. 'You think you can get away with it?'

'Why not? That old fool Tannadyce won't give any trouble. As for Hewitt, we'll leave him out of this. After the way he showed up at that trial, I reckon we can't afford to trust him too far. Not that he can do us any harm, but he may become obstructive.'

'All right, I'll witness it. I only hope you know what you're doing.'

'Fine.' Klagge sounded hearty. 'Then you'll be the sheriff from now on, Laredo, with Jose here as your deputy.'

'And what do we do with Duprey and that deputy of his?' leered Laredo.

Klagge thought a moment, then stared down at the redly glowing tip of his cigar. 'Ride 'em both out of town,' he grated. 'That way, we'll be rid of 'em for good.' He glanced at the lawyer as he spoke.

'Suits me,' said Corday.

'Then see to it right away,' muttered Klagge to the two grinning men near the door. 'But don't be too hard on 'em.'

★　★　★

Neither Laredo nor Jose could fully suppress their elation at the turn of events. It was a situation neither had anticipated, but they now intended to exploit it to the full. There had, in the past, been several men in town who had looked down on them while they had been merely range-hands riding for Klagge. Now all of that was over. They had positions of power in the town and, with Klagge backing their play, there seemed little anybody else could do about it.

Laredo stood in front of the small cell, peering in at the two men seated on the low bunk. 'All right, Duprey,' he said, thinly. 'On your feet. Both of you!'

Slowly, Duprey stood up. He glared at the other through the bars. 'What's wrong?' he asked harshly. 'Come to mete out the same kind of horse justice for us now that you've hanged Corrie?'

Laredo's lips flattened over his teeth as he unlocked the door and swung it wide, stepping back a little, his hand close to his Colt. 'Better watch your mouth, Duprey. You're talkin' to the new sheriff now.'

Duprey looked stolidly at the other's leering face as he moved past him, hesitated, not knowing whether to laugh or not, then he merely shrugged. 'I suppose I might have known Klagge would have to do somethin' like this to keep the town in check while he takes over everythin'. But I sure wouldn't like to be in your boots when the town finds out what's really happenin'.'

Still grinning, Loredo swung his arm. His clenched fist connected solidly with the side of Duprey's face, sending him crashing helplessly against the iron bars of the cell.

'We've got our orders to ride you out of town, both of you.' Laredo's voice was sharply vicious. 'Only we weren't told how we were to do it. So we just figured out a way that'll make sure you don't come back.'

Jose came into the passage from the direction of the outer office. 'You having any trouble with them prisoners, Laredo?' he asked.

'Nothin' I can't handle.' Laredo stepped forward, twisted Duprey's arm right up the middle of his back, lifting him half on to his toes, pushing him along the passage behind the deputy.

'Get their mounts from across the street, Jose,' he said, as he thrust Duprey towards the street door. 'Bring a couple of ropes, too. I'll be needin' them.'

'You got somethin' in mind for these *hombres*?' inquired Jose softly.

'You'll see when you get those horses here.'

The half-breed returned with them three minutes later. He held them steady while Laredo secured the ends of the ropes to the saddlehorns. When he had finished, he motioned Duprey and the deputy forward. 'This is not going to be pleasant ride out of town,' he said, his tone very soft, 'but reckon it will be one to remember.' Out of the corner of his eye, he saw that Klagge and Corday had come out of the hotel and were standing on the boardwalk watching the proceedings. 'Keep them covered while I tie their legs,' he said to the half-breed.

'What the hell you goin' to do?' demanded George harshly. He looked at Duprey with an expression of apprehensive fear in his eyes.

'They figure on lettin' the horses drag us out of town,' said Duprey tonelessly. 'It's the sort of thing that amuses men like this.'

'You want to be thankful that our orders are to let you live,' snarled Jose fiercely. He felt his finger tighten momentarily on the trigger, wondered if he could claim they had been trying to escape if he was to tighten his finger just a shade. Then he forced himself to relax. This was going to be just as good. A bullet would be far too quick and clean.

Bending, Laredo tied the ropes securely around the men's ankles, gave them a tug to be sure the knots would hold, then stepped carefully back, throwing a quick glance up and down the street.

There were several bystanders along the boardwalks, watching what was going on. It was impossible to read from their faces what they were thinking, but nobody had made a move to stop them and now it was too late anyway. He moved a couple of yards away, then pulled out his gun and fired two shots into the air, spooking the horses. Within seconds the slack ropes had tautened, whipping the two men off their feet, hauling them along the dusty street behind the madly careering horses.

Laredo stood and watched as the dust settled slowly, then turned to Jose. 'I reckon it's about time we had a drink,' he said emotionlessly. 'Being the sheriff is mighty dry work around here.'

★ ★ ★

Frank and the girl came upon timber an hour after leaving Fresno City, and there was a narrow trail branching off the main trail across the desert, running upgrade into the pine country. Stella sat like a man in the saddle, her stirrups low, her legs thrust straight down, her slender, lissom body swaying in unison with the movements of the horse. Once, as they swung off the trail to the right, striking into the hills, she turned to look at him as if some sudden thought had crossed her mind, compelling her. Then she looked back again, lips pressed together. They rode up to the summit of the trail. Ahead of them it dipped and wound in a series of smooth curves, cutting in and out of the lone, slender pines with, here and there, a faint glint of water catching the light of the sun where it filtered down into small clearings.

Here the girl stopped, reining up her mount smoothly. She pointed off to the right, beyond the sloping curve of the hill. 'The Lazy T is in that direction,' she said. 'There is only the one trail leading to it, that which we just left down there.'

'What about this one?' Frank asked.

'I'll show you that. It comes to a dead end a quarter of a mile from here, even though it doesn't look like it from up here. There's a cabin there at the very end where an old friend of my father's lives. His name's Clark Forrester. Don't ask me why he prefers to stay up here in such seclusion. I've heard him say that he prefers the company of animals to human beings, but whether that's anything to do with it, I don't know. Anyway, he makes an excellent sentinel. From there he can watch the trail for several miles, and can give us warning of anyone riding against us.'

'Did he see that posse?'

'Yes. But he knew there would be real trouble when he saw Sheriff Duprey riding with them. If it had been Klagge alone, he would have passed the word to us.'

She went on, crossed a narrow stream that came down from somewhere in the higher hills, then through a wide clearing, keeping to the trail that wound among the trees, the floor of the forest covered by a thick carpet of pine needles that muffled the sound of their horses.

Even so, as they broke cover and rode into the wider clearing on the very edge of the hillside, the man standing in the doorway of the log cabin had evidently been waiting for them. He came forward as they reined up. A couple of lean dogs snuffled in the grass near the cabin and there was a horse grazing on the edge of the clearing.

The man was tall, well over six feet in

height, and thin, which made him seem even taller. He had a hatchet-face, cleft-chin, and eyes set a little too close to the pinched nose for good looks. His voice, when he spoke, sounded old and tired and it was impossible, from his voice or his face, to say how old he was.

'Saw you riding this way, Stella,' he said. 'You want some coffee? Got it on the stove right now.'

'Thanks, Clark. We could use some.'

They dismounted and followed the other into the cabin. The clearing acted as a heat trap and even in the shack it was unbearably hot, and the stove in the middle glowed a faint red. As he took the mug of steaming coffee from the other, Forrester laid a bare glance on Frank, eyeing him appraisingly. It was a look that seemed to cut right through him, baring his soul to the man's searching gaze.

'You riding for Stella's father?'

'That's right. Signed on for him a couple of days ago.'

'Hope for your sake you're no

newcomer to trouble.' As he spoke, Clark turned to the girl. 'There's a feel in the hills these days, Stella. Somethin' is goin' to break. It's like the quiet you get just before a thunderstorm hits the summits. Saw the sheriff and his men ride through day before yesterday. What'd they want at the Lazy T?'

'They came to try to arrest me,' Frank said quietly.

'Was that Duprey's doing, or Klagge's?'

'It was Klagge's,' put in the girl from the other side of the room. 'We had some trouble in town this morning. They tried to hang Frank here.'

'I can understand that,' Forrester nodded. Again that sharp-bright glance was laid on Frank. 'You've got the look of a gunfighter about you. Plain to see. Klagge won't like it if you help Kent. He aims to have the Lazy T for his own, and all of the water that goes with it.'

'That's how we figured it,' Frank replied. He looked out through the door. 'You've certainly got an excellent view of the trail from up here. I wager you could see for twenty miles on a clear day.'

Clark grinned. 'Not only that, but there's a natural bend here in the hills that carries the sound up from the valley. I can pick out a single rider more'n three miles away in either direction.'

'Clark has been very useful to us in the past, passing on warnings whenever Klagge has tried to surprise us, or rustle our cattle. I think we would have been finished long before now if it hadn't been for him.'

'And doesn't Klagge even suspect what's going on?'

'It wouldn't appear so,' said Forrester. He drained his mug and placed it on top of the stove.

Stella laid her mug down too, moved to the door. 'Better keep a sharp look-out from now on, Clark. After what happened in town today, Klagge will be ready to swing in every man he has against us.'

'I'll be ready.'

Swinging up into the saddle, Stella led the way downgrade, back to the main trail. She did not speak again until they were within sight of the ranch. 'Clark Forrester is one of the few men we can rely on implicitly. We can always turn to him for help. He knows most of the men in the hills and several in the town, too. If it came to a real showdown with Klagge, he may be able to swing them all behind us.'

'I'd like to have another talk with him soon. Maybe I'll ride out tonight.'

She eyed him closely. For a moment there seemed to be a question weighed in her mind. Then she thrust it away, rode silently into the courtyard.

6

Black Treachery

Frank reined his horse and made a wide circle of the Lazy T ranch before striking east towards the distant hills, where he hoped to find Clark Forrester. The main trail was a solid streak of dust, glowing faintly in the shadowy dusk, easily followed. For a little while he allowed the horse to pick its own pace, then pushed it on with a greater urgency. The silence that lay in the hills was filled with a suppressed tension that seemed, to him, to be a signal of things to come. Austen Klagge would not be standing still after what had happened in town. What had happened to Duprey and his deputy, he did not know. There was always the chance that Klagge had been so incensed by losing him that he had strung up both men as a warning; but somehow he doubted that. Klagge was an ambitious and utterly ruthless man and he would kill to gain his own ends, but he was not a fool. He knew that at the moment, until he had gained full control of the territory around Fresno City, he would have to tread warily as far as public opinion went. He could not afford to set the people of the town against him, as he undoubtedly would if he hanged those two lawmen.

As he rode he turned his thoughts to Stella Michener. The picture of her in his mind evoked a feeling of warmth and satisfaction, something new to him as far as women were concerned. Although she seemed cold and distant towards him, he had the unshakable impression that there was a human warmth and depth to her character which she had shown on only a few rare occasions.

He was four miles along the trail when he picked out the sound of hoofbeats ahead of him, coming along slowly. Turning off the trail, he waited until the two shadowy figures drew level with him, then moved the bay out on to the trail, the Colt levelled on the men. He saw their mounts shy up at his presence, saw the pale blurs of the men's faces as they swung to face him.

'Who's that?' asked a voice.

Still keeping the two men covered, Frank gigged his horse forward, then lowered the gun. 'Frank Corrie,' he said quietly.

The nearer man leaned sideways in the saddle, stared at him closely in surprise. 'How the hell did you get away? We figured you were dead when Klagge's men dragged you out of jail.'

Pouching the Colt, Frank said: 'Some of the Lazy T boys were in town and managed to put a stop to that. But what happened to you?' Now that he came to look more closely at the two men, he was able to see their pitiful condition. Their clothing was torn and streaked with blood and dust, their faces lacerated, the sleeves torn from their jackets and shirts, exposing their arms.

Duprey grinned mirthlessly. 'Laredo Ford was made sheriff by Klagge and Corday,' he said tonelessly. 'They took us from the jail and hitched us by ropes to a couple of horses and sent them dragging us out of town.' Bitterly, he continued: 'They must've figured it would learn us not to come back. I guess they badly underestimated us. We're headed for the Lazy T. Maybe Kent Michener could use another couple of guns.'

'Hell, man, you're both half dead.' It seemed incredible to Frank that either man could still be alive after their experience.

'Looks worse than it really is,' said the other man harshly. 'Besides, we've now got a big score to settle with Klagge, and we reckon this is the best way of doing it.'

'You got any idea what Klagge intends doin' now?'

Duprey hesitated, rubbed his chin, wincing visibly as his fingers touched the deep cuts where the blood had mingled with the sweat and the dirt, congealing around his mouth and along his cheeks. 'He can do almost anything now with Laredo as sheriff.'

Frank nodded. 'You'd better get along to the ranch and get those injuries tended to. I've got a chore to do, but I'll keep my eyes open in case Klagge does decide to ride against Michener tonight.'

'They could come pussyfooting it across the desert and hit you before you knew they were there,' put in the deputy.

'I doubt it,' said Frank confidently. Wheeling his mount, he raked spurs along its flanks. Not until he reached the low foothills did he go forward with caution, observing that everything was quiet here, a little too quiet for his liking. Even the whippoorwills were silent among the trees. When he reached the point where the narrow trail wound up from the valley, he stopped in the shadows of the trees to scan the terrain about him. Nothing moved as far as the eye could see and yet there was a faint tingling along the small hairs on the nape of his neck, a warning signal he had learned from past experience never to ignore.

This country round about the hills was full of dodgers, men on the run hiding themselves away from the main haunts of men, shunning company, keeping themselves to themselves, not daring to move out for fear of bumping up against the law.

It was not in him to wait. Deliberately he rode his mount up the winding trail to the summit and then down in the series of switchback curves to the wide clearing overlooking the valley some two hundred feet below. The cabin glimmered faintly in the pale moonlight that slanted down through breaks in the thick canopy of leaves closing in over the trail. He reined up at the edge of the clearing, swung down from the saddle and moved noiselessly forward on foot. There was a faint light showing through the window of the cabin and around the side of the partly opened door.

'Clark,' he called softly as he approached the door. He hesitated when there was no reply. The feeling that there was something very wrong was strong within him; something he could sense but not define. Drawing the Colt from its holster, he thumbed back the hammer and pushed open the door quietly, stepping into the cabin. The stale smell of the place came out to him; a blend of rancid fat and meat. At first he saw nothing. It was as if Forrester had just left the place and gone out for a few moments. He felt a slight sense of relief. Then something moved over in the corner, and by the flickering light from the lantern on the high table he saw the bared fangs of one of the dogs. It came forward slowly, sliding on its belly, eyes glistening in the dimness.

'Steady, boy,' he said softly. 'Everythin's going to be all right.'

He held the gun tightly, gently releasing the hammer. The next second the dog leapt at him, fangs reaching for his throat. Instinctively he side-stepped, felt the muzzle brush against the side of his face as he brought the barrel of the gun hard down on the animal's skull. It collapsed with a whimper at his feet.

Moving carefully around it, he advanced into the room. His foot touched something soft and yielding that lay on the other side of the table in the shadow thrown by it. Glancing down, he saw that his sense of danger had not been wrong.

Swiftly he bent beside the inert form, turning the man over. Forrester stared sightlessly at the ceiling, eyes wide. There was a thin trickle of dried blood at the corner of his mouth and more staining the back of his shirt. It felt sodden and sticky under his fingers. A quick investigation told him that it was not a bullet wound in the other's back. Forrester had been knifed.

Hunching back on his heels, Frank

thought fast. Evidently the girl's belief that Klagge knew nothing of Forrester's role in the defence of the Lazy T ranch had been ill founded. How long Klagge had known it was impossible to say. But on this occasion he had played his cards well. Someone must have crept up to the window of the cabin and thrown that knife with an unerring aim; someone who did not want to make any sound at all and had therefore not risked using a gun.

Swiftly he turned over the possibilities in his mind. There was just the chance that Forrester had had enemies, even among the hill folk of this area, and one of them had seized the opportunity of doing this. But it was the more urgent and ominous possibility that dominated his mind. With Forrester dead, killed before he could give any warning to Kent Michener, the Lazy T ranch and everyone there was in deadly danger. Klagge and his killers could sweep down on it unexpectedly and overrun the defenders.

Without pausing to think any further, he went outside, climbed swiftly into the saddle and rode back down the treacherous trail at breakneck speed.

★　★　★

Not more than twenty minutes before Frank arrived at the cabin in the clearing, Jose Rand had slipped stealthily out of the place, wiping the blade of the slender-handled knife on the grass in the clearing before making his way to the far side where his mount was tethered. Unlike Frank, he did not return to the valley by the narrow trail, but put his horse to the steep downgrade where the trees thinned out and there was a narrow rocky ledge straddling the precipitous slope. It was a highly dangerous method of descent and on several occasions the horse went down on to its knees, almost pitching him out of the saddle and over its head. But somehow they made it down to the valley where Austen Klagge and the others were waiting in a small cut-off to one side of the main trail.

'Did you finish the job?' Klagge asked harshly.

Jose grinned, his teeth a white flash in his shadowed features. 'He's dead,' he said tersely. 'He won't be passin' on any more warnin's to Michener.'

'Good. Then let's ride. The sooner we get this chore done the better I'll like it. If we hit them hard enough tonight, the Lazy T could be mine this time tomorrow.'

They headed out of the cut-off at a slow run, then increased the gait of their mounts as they hit the desert, leaving behind the slow-settling dust streamers in the still moonlit night air.

★ ★ ★

Kent Michener stood on the porch of the ranch, staring out into the moonlit darkness, dredging his thoughts, trying to make something out of them. He had been only half surprised when Frank

Corrie had ridden off shortly after sundown, saying he was going up into the hills to have a talk with Forrester. There was something about Corrie that he did not quite understand and he wished that he knew what it was, for he was convinced it was important. Had he heard the other's name somewhere before, somewhere in the past? It seemed unlikely. The chances were that it was borrowed like the names of so many of the men who rode through these parts. Some stayed on here and others just kept on going, heading for California and the illusion of prosperity which beckoned from the Golden State.

And what did the other want with Clark? There was no answer in his mind to that, but both men could look after themselves, and he turned his attention to more immediate and pressing problems. The news he had received from Duprey concerning Klagge making Laredo Ford the new sheriff was disturbing. With that man in office, Klagge virtually ran the town. He had everyone there under his thumb. They could be arrested and tossed into jail on the slightest pretext. Indeed, there did not even have to be any reason. Naturally, Klagge would go easily at first, but once he found his feet, knew where his friends were, and how many enemies he might have, he would be far more bold.

Lighting a cigar, he leaned on the rail of the porch, letting his gaze wander over the bunkhouse and the corral, the grazing land on the lee of the hill which over-looked the valley. All of this he had built with his own hands, it was almost all he had in the world; an infinitely precious thing to a man such as himself; and now it was all threatened with destruction by the greed of one man.

For a moment the anger that rose in him directed against Austen Klagge almost overwhelmed him. Then, with a supreme effort, he forced it down. He thought of Emma, who lay in her grave on the side of the hill. She had died almost seven years before but her memory was still as fresh in his thoughts as it had been then. No, he reflected tiredly, this was where he had put down his roots and they would have to kill him before he would relinquish his hold on it.

Taking the heavy Colt from its holster — for he had buckled on his gunbelt when he had heard the news from town — he looked down at it with a sudden sense of loss. He had hoped that the old ways of violence were finished in this part of the territory. It was all wrong that a weapon such as this should be necessary to preserve a man's heritage. He had hoped that Stella would marry some day, that she would inherit all of this, build it up even further. Now that was all threatened and —

The faint sound in the distance had not, at first, caught his attention. Now it did, caught it and held it. It was the clatter of shod hoofs on rock as the approaching riders came over the trail at the top of the hill. Then there was silence with only the tell-tale edges of sound whispering through it. The riders had not halted. They had merely ridden off the trail on to the muffling grass at the edges of the trail. This alone pointed to the fact that they were not riders coming for a social call. He swiftly stubbed out the cigar and moved back into the house, slamming the door behind him.

At the table, Stella looked up in sudden surprise, a faint expression of alarm on her face.

'Father! What is it?'

'Klagge and his men. I'm sure of it. I heard them crossing the top of the hill. Then they rode out on to the grass so as not to be heard.'

'But surely Clark would have — '

Grabbing a rifle from the wall, Michener opened one of the drawers in the nearby desk, broke open the packet of shells he found there, spilling them out in front of him, thrusting them into the weapon. There was a grimness on his face that came not only from the fact that Klagge's men were out there, moving in rapidly on the ranch. but from the new thought which had just struck him, searing like a flame through his mind. He murmured tightly: 'Clark wouldn't be able to warn us if someone rode out and got to him first.'

From the look in Stella's eyes, he saw that the same thought that had flashed through his mind had also occurred to her. 'You mean Frank,' she said harshly, her hand at her throat. 'You think he could have done this?'

'It makes sense, doesn't it? I was always a little uncertain of that man. Funny he wanted to ride out and talk with Forrester tonight, so soon after he'd met up with him. He met Duprey on the trail and there was no sign of Klagge then.'

'But they were going to hang him when we interfered,' she protested. Her mind was whirling. Part of her said that he could have done this while the rest murmured that there had to be some other explanation of this. But there was little time in which to try to puzzle it out now.

Moments later, after warning the other men in the house, they had taken up their places near the windows. The lamps had been extinguished and the place was in total darkness, with only the flooding moonlight outside to give them light to see by.

Michener raised his gun and waited impatiently for his first target to come into sight. When it did, the man was careful to stay out of range of a killing shot. In the moonlight, he thought it was Laredo Ford, but he could not be sure. The light made details tricky and the other, after running forward a couple of yards, had thrown himself down out of sight behind the horse trough on the edge of the corral.

Michener waited and the time passed slowly. He blinked his eyes several times to adjust them to the dimness outside.

'Michener!'

Kent looked up at the sudden

unexpected call of his name. He watched the spot where he had seen the other go down, feeling the smooth hardness of the window ledge against his arms, and did not answer.

'Michener! This is the sheriff. I'm going to give you a chance to walk out of there alive and with your hands in the air. That goes for all of the men with you, especially Corrie. I guess you know the penalty for aidin' and harbourin' a wanted murderer, not to say helpin' him to escape from the law.'

'If you're talkin' about Corrie, then he ain't here,' Kent called back.

There was a brief pause, then a voice he recognized as Rand's called out from a different direction. 'We know you're lying, Michener. You've got half a minute to make your decision. Then we'll blast this place apart.'

'Go to hell!' Michener roared. He tightened his finger on the trigger as he saw the crown of a hat appear hesitantly above the trough. He was ready to fire when he saw it tilt awkwardly and knew that it was balanced on the barrel of a sixgun, designed to draw his fire and give away his position. His finger relaxed on the trigger.

'Hold your fire,' he said in a low whisper to the others. 'They'll be waitin' to rush us. Probably workin' their way around the place while Laredo is out there drawin' our attention.'

'We've got men posted at all of the windows, Father,' said Stella. Her tone was even and steady, without a tremor. Lifting his head cautiously, Kent Michener stared out into the stillness of the night. Every muscle in him was so tight, stretched to its physical limit, that he ached all over.

A rifle shot cracked in the stillness and echoed thinly in the split through the hills. Then another, as the men in the bunkhouse opened up. Seconds later a full volley crashed out from the men surrounding the ranch. Somebody yelled in the darkness and the entire house shook as another blast of gunfire tore through the windows. Glass splintered into the room as Michener drew himself back, dropping full length on to the floor as the bullets from Klagge's party crashed into the room. Wood splintered above him. He felt a strangely creepy feeling about this and a small amount of panic threatened to tear through him, making him roll on one side and jerk his feet away from the wall, as though expecting lead to penetrate the thick wood and stone.

Gently he levered himself up on to one knee and risked a quick look outside. A man ran from the direction of the trees towards the corral, a shadowy figure, bent and doubled over to present a more difficult target. Jerking up the gun, he aimed quickly and fired, saw the man stumble, put out his hands in front of himself, then recover and run on. Before he could squeeze off another shot, Stella had fired. The man ran on for another couple of yards, arms and legs flailing wildly as the bullet hit him. Then he tilted forward and went down, sliding on his knees before coming to a halt, bending forward from the middle until he lay on his face in the grey-shining dust. Very slowly his body relaxed and lay still.

Behind the horse trough Laredo lay flat on his stomach. He was keenly aware of the fact that he was pinned down now, and after seeing what had happened to Charlie Kratz, who lay on his face only a few feet away, he knew it would be suicide to try to move from his present position. But the rest of the men were pouring a steady fire into the house from all sides now, shifting the weight of their fire from time to time, keeping the defenders on the hop, never knowing from one minute to the next from which direction the main assault would come.

All they had to do now was keep up the fire for a little while to soften up those inside the ranchhouse and the bunkhouse nearby and then rush them from three sides at once. Out of the corner of his eye, he watched the brief orange stilettos of flame from the edge of the courtyard. Most of the men were clustered there with only a few at the back of the place, but from there it was possible to pour a deadly crossfire into both buildings without exposing themselves too much.

A revolver shot whined down from the front of the ranch, the bullet kicking up dust within a couple of inches of his face. Cursing, he realized he had shifted his position slightly, exposing himself. Drawing back, he aimed several shots at the window from which the gunfire had come, fanning the hammer, ripping off the shots so quickly that the sound was one continuous roll. In the echoing roar he heard a man give up a loud cry, and grinned fiendishly to himself as he ducked back under cover.

Somewhere in the distance he heard Klagge yelling at the men, and from the corner of his vision saw a small group of them run off to the right, heading for the barn. Revolver shots followed them from the bunkhouse and two men fell, but the rest faded into the dim interior.

A moment later Klagge's voice came again: 'You all right, Laredo?'

'Sure.'

'Keep their heads down while the boys get ready to burn 'em out.'

Slowly then, Laredo wriggled along the ground, moving on his elbows, snakelike, to the end of the trough. Pausing there, he thumbed more shells into the Colt. Klagge's plan was clear now. There was bound to be a hay wagon in the barn someplace. Once a torch was put to it, the men could send it rolling down to the ranch house. The thought sparked off a slow rise of vicious anticipation in Laredo's mind. That should smoke 'em out right enough, he thought. Either they come running out into the open or they stayed there and fried. He hoped that, in spite of all that might happen, the girl would be taken alive. He had his own plans for her. She had been one of those who looked down on him, despising him. It would give him the greatest pleasure in the world to take her and break that proud spirit once and for all.

Firing burst out once more with a sultry violence from the house as the men inside saw their danger. A man standing just inside the door of the barn wrapped both of his arms tightly around his belly, howling with pain as he staggered from one side to the other. Behind him there was a faint flash of flame as one of the others lit a match and applied it to the side of the straw on the wagon. The straw, tinder-dry, caught at once, blazing up fiercely. In the vivid glare, the figures of the four men inside the barn were clearly visible, struggling to push the wagon out through the narrow doorway and on to the gentle slope that would carry it down towards the house which lay directly in its path.

★　★　★

As Frank Corrie rode through the pines on top of the hill that overlooked the wide valley, the savage break of gunfire came to him, borne along by the faint breeze that had sprung up. His way had been upgrade for a mile or so and he had pushed the bay at a punishing pace, so that it was now labouring as they crossed the summit and dipped downward. As the pines thinned out, Frank reined up and paused for a brief moment to consider the proposition. If he rode straight down into the courtyard, he ran the risk of being among those men before he was aware of it. If he delayed and edged around them, taking them from the rear, then he might be too late. It was one of those quick decisions, ended immediately.

Swinging down from the saddle on the run, he grabbed at the Winchester and then raced forward into the moon-thrown shadows, gliding silently from one concealing patch of darkness to another. The din of the gunfire, bucketing through the night, drowned out any small sounds he might make. He ran along the edge of the flat meadow two hundred yards from the bunkhouse, eyes alert, his gaze switching from side to side, watchful for any sign of movement.

The sound of voices, carrying well on the breeze, stopped him abruptly in his tracks. Crouching down, he levered a shell into the breech of the Winchester, wriggled forward through the tall grass. A volley crashed down on the house, the air shaking with the thunderous cannonade. All of this was in front of him, a play of shadows in the pale moonlight. Studying the situation, he cast a quick, all-encompassing glance about him.

Austen Klagge had his men in a ring around the beleaguered ranch house, was able to bring fire to bear from any direction. There was also a man lying near the corral, just beyond a body sprawled out in the open. From where he lay, somewhat above the courtyard, he could catch the occasional spurt of flame from the man's gun.

He turned his head slowly and it was then that he saw the feverish activity that was taking place just inside the wide-open door of the barn facing the southern wall of the ranch house. The brief flare of flame passed so swiftly that he thought he had been mistaken. Then there came the sweeping orange glow as straw or some similar material caught fire. The plan was fiendishly clear. Some gunfire was coming from the house, but Frank could see that the gunmen there could never hope to hit the men so long as they remained inside the barn. In split seconds Frank was literally hurtling down the slope, feet slipping in the grass and small stones. He never knew how it was he escaped being hit by the intense defensive fire from the ranch. Ten feet from the edge of the courtyard, with the barn less than twenty yards away, the tall shape of a man suddenly rose up from the long grass in front of him.

Frank had a momentary glimpse of

the thin face, the half-open mouth, and the Colt swinging slowly to cover him, finger tightening on the trigger. The man must have recognized him for he turned to yell a warning. He plunged forward at the man. Both went down, the other uttering a choked cry as the gun was knocked from his fingers, jarred from his outflung hand as he hit the ground.

Frank was on top of the man. The other's bony hands came up, clawing for his throat, clamping a tight hold around it, squeezing remorselessly. The unexpected strength in those taloned fingers was an unpleasant surprise to Frank. He felt as if his eyes were bulging out of their sockets and there was the continual throbbing of the blood locked in his head, growing worse with each passing second as the other increased the murderous pressure on his windpipe.

The roaring in his head was a vast waterfall of thunder, clamouring within his skull. The constricting band around his chest, drawing tighter over his ribs, indicated that his lungs were rapidly becoming starved for air. He swung his left hand, hammering at the other's head, but the blow seemed to have little effect. The man merely grimaced and pressed his thumbs harder into Frank's throat, seeking to cut off his air altogether.

With a tremendous effort, he lifted his legs, then brought his knees down hard on the other's unprotected stomach, using the whole of his weight in the attempt. The gunman gasped as all of the wind was knocked from his body. His hold on Frank's throat relaxed a little and he jerked his head back sharply. The other's grip did not loosen completely, but the move forced the other's head up off the ground, and as Frank thrust his own head forward, the other's skull struck the hard ground with a sickening thud, and a thin bleat of agony was forced from his lips. Savagely Frank tore his throat away from the other's powerful hands, swung his clenched fist at the man's unprotected jaw and, with a harsh, choking groan, the man's head snapped back and he lay still.

Frank rolled clear, grabbed at the Winchester, breathing deeply for a few moments. His head was still throbbing violently, but he forced himself to his feet and ran on, across the courtyard, until he reached the wall of the barn on one side of the open door. He could hear the curses of the men inside as they manhandled the bulky wagon, which was blazing fiercely. It was evident that they had not taken into account the difficulties inherent in manoeuvring a wagon in the confined space.

Already sparks from the burning straw was the main danger. Several smouldering patches of flame were already showing inside the barn. There was no time to make any plans. At any moment those men would succeed in getting the burning wagon through the doorway, and once that happened, nothing on earth would prevent it from smashing into the side of the ranch.

Levelling the Winchester on the men, he snapped: 'Hold it right there. One funny move from anyone and that man dies.'

'It's Corrie,' muttered one of the men standing near the wagon.

'So it's Corrie,' said another man standing near the far side of the wagon. Frank recognized Jose Rand, the half-breed. 'He's only one man and there are four of us. He can't get us all. And with that rifle, he'll be pretty slow in getting off his shots.' There was an ice-cold glitter in the sunken eyes. 'Draw on him and gun him down.'

Frank grinned confidently, allowed his gaze to wander from one man to the other. He noted the false front of three of the men. Only the half-breed looked dangerous. There was no trace of hesitancy or doubt on the man's face, only the chilling look of a man with many a bloody gunfight behind him. Only the fact that he recognized he would be the first to get a bullet stopped him from going for his gun right there. But he would be ready if any of his companions decided to try.

'Now drop your gunbelts, left-handed. Walk out of here with your hands lifted, and if any of you think I'm bluffing, then he can go for his gun right now.' He was playing a dangerous game but if he could break their apparently united front, get three of them to fold up, he knew he could take Rand if he did decide to act. Frank's confidence in the face of seemingly overwhelming odds had its effect on the men in front of him; that and the fact that he was standing between them and the doorway and, at their backs, the flames were flaring higher from the wagon they had set alight. They had a choice to make and very little time in which to make it. Obey him and surrender, or stay there and either be burned to death or get a bullet.

'You can't stop us alone, Corrie, no matter how fast you are,' leered Rand.

He shifted his stance a little, eyes narrowed down. His right hand was swinging slowly very close to the butt of his Colt.

Still keeping his eyes fixed on Rand, Frank said tersely: 'If you men are backing his play, go ahead. I can take two of you at least with me. Maybe more. Now shuck those gunbelts or reach for your guns.'

The seconds ticked by and still the three men paused. There was a sheen of sweat on their faces, not all of which was brought on by the stifling heat and smoke inside the barn. Reluctantly, using their left hands, the three men unbuckled their gunbelts and let them fall.

Rand's ugly eyes were riveted on Frank's face. He knew what their actions meant and his rage seemed to engulf him completely. 'Get the hell out of here. I don't need you yeller-livered gringos to back any play I make,' he roared.

Frank was aware of the men sidling

out of the barn. A moment after they had gone there was the scuffing of their feet in the dust as they ran across the courtyard. The volume of gunfire from the ranch rose to a crescendo. Frank heard death come to one of the men in a stuttering gasp, the thud of lead ripping through flesh, bone and sinew. But not for a second did he take his eyes off the man who faced him.

At Rand's back the fire was spreading swiftly. The wagon was a mass of flames, forcing the half-breed to move further from it, and the flames were rapidly engulfing the back of the building. The wooden structure, the planks tinder-dry from the long period of drought, were beginning to flare like a great torch, and even Frank knew that there would be nothing any one could do to save it from total destruction. Rand was now crouched back, his silhouette outlined against the flames, his face, in the glaring light, glistening redly with sweat. Within minutes the place would be an inferno.

Rand's eyes dropped to the Winchester levelled on him. 'You goin' to shoot me down in cold blood, Corrie?'

'In the present circumstances, I think I'd be perfectly justified in doin' just that,' Frank retorted tightly.

'You wouldn't do it,' said Rand. 'I know your type. You have to believe that you're faster than the other man. They tell me you're a fast man with a gun. Let's see just how fast you really are.'

Deliberately Frank dropped the rifle on to the straw at his feet, faced the other man down. He saw the first break of uncertainty on the half-breed's smooth features.

'All right,' he said evenly. 'Now we're even. Go for your gun any time you like. This is your play.'

Rand ran the tip of his tongue across his lips. In spite of his earlier words, he felt that somehow he had faced the wrong man. Most of his past killings had been against men he knew to be slow with a gun, or men too drunk to handle a Colt: but the steely-eyed man in front of him, his face lit by the flickering flare of the flames, was a totally different proposition to any of these, and his gunman's courage was beginning to fail him.

'Well,' said Frank, as the other continued to hesitate. 'What are you waitin' for? Gettin' set to talk me to death?'

The half-breed's gaze flickered for just a second, staring over Frank's left shoulder. A moment later a harsh voice said: 'What the hell's goin' on in here, Jose? Why haven't you got that god-damn wagon rollin' yet?'

Instinctively, warned by some intuitive sense, Frank whirled away from the wall. He felt the sudden burst of heat on his face and neck, then heard the sudden explosion of a Colt behind him. The slug fanned his cheek, struck the burning upright of the wagon, sending a splinter of smouldering wood flying into the rear of the barn. Out of the corner of his eye, as he flung himself down on to the floor, he saw Rand claw for his gun, his hand slashing down towards the holster, dragging the weapon from its holster, bringing up the barrel in a gleaming arc to level it on his body. He knew it needed only a quick snap of the wrist for that gun to come to bear on him, the finger tightening instinctively on the trigger, to send a slug burning its way into his body. As he went for his own gun, he knew that he ought to have shot the half-breed down while there had been the opportunity.

The flaring gouts of fire that spewed from the two guns came at almost the same instant and the barn resounded deafeningly to the roar of the gunfire. Lying on one elbow. Frank fired three point-blank shots before he felt himself driven back against the wall of the barn under the driving impact of a slug in his arm. A red wall of agony fogged his vision, blending with the smoke and flame which now seemed to be all around him, ringing him in with a solid wall. Sweat trickled into his eyes, half blinding him. In spite of the pain in his left arm, he dashed the back of his hand across his forehead, wiping away the perspiration, clenched his teeth and waited for death to come. No bullet came out of the grey smoke. Dimly, he peered into the blazing holocaust.

A dim figure was just visible near the burning tongue of the wagon where it rested on the floor of the barn. It was Jose Rand, bent forward almost in an attitude of prayer, sobbing, with lead buried deep within his body, the life ebbing swiftly from him.

Very slowly, his features corroded with pain, the half-breed tried to force himself to straighten up. He still held the Colt in the fingers of his right hand, but there was blood soaking into his shirt and, in the harsh light of the flames, Frank could see the red and ugly holes in his chest. Rand was staring directly at him, eyes wide, lips thinned back across his teeth with the tremendous physical effort he was making. Now he was on his knees, swaying slightly, striving with fierce determination to lift the Colt, which seemed to be far too heavy for him. Slowly it came up, the barrel lifting, the effort costing him dearly.

Sucking a great gust of air down into his lungs, forcing himself to ignore the pain which lanced through his left arm, Frank waited until the other's gun was almost levelled on him, then fired two shots at point blank range into the half-breed's heart. Jose Rand fell backward on to the burning straw. He was dead before his shoulders hit the ground.

As he stared unseeingly at the dead man, Frank was vaguely aware of the babble of voices outside the barn. But it was impossible to make out the words, or who the men were, above the crackle of the flames as they swept avidly through the building and the thunderous roar of the blood pumping along his veins. Everything seemed to be taking place at a great distance from him.

Screwing up his eyes, he tried to see, but all that showed in front of his blurred vision were a couple of wavering figures standing in the door-way, their features indistinguishable.

'Get him out of there,' a loud voice boomed. 'The whole place is gone, anyway. We can't hope to save it.'

Frank had only time to recognize Kent Michener's voice, to have a moment in which to wonder how the other came to be there, and then he slumped down on the burning, bloody floor, and everything became foggy and indistinct.

7

Dark Sundown

Frank Corrie recovered consciousness with the bitter taste of something resembling decaying wood in his mouth. Weakly, he opened his eyes, tried to turn his head to look about him, but everything he saw was unfamiliar. He shivered slightly, lifted his head, but was forced to let it drop on to the pillow again as pain stabbed viciously through his skull, pulsing at the back of his eyes.

He tested his physical condition a few moments later by trying to sit up, but it was too much of an effort, and he buckled back on to the bed. There was, he noticed, the faint glow of sunlight coming in through the half-open window, and it was cool and quiet in the room. Lying back, staring up at the ceiling, he tried to call back memory, to think out what had happened. His left arm and shoulder felt stiff and when he tried to move them he felt some form of restriction. Fumbling with his right hand, he felt the bandage which swathed the whole of his upper arm and winced as the touch of his fingers brought pain.

There was the sense of having been unconscious for a long period of time and, screwing up his eyes, he tried to estimate the time of day from the slant of the sun's rays through the window. But there was no way of telling whether it was the day after the attack on the Lazy T ranch, or several days after.

Five minutes later he heard the door of the bedroom open and, lowering his eyes, staring across the sheets over his body, he saw Stella Michener come into the room. For a moment there was a look of concern on her face, then, as she saw he was awake, she smiled and there was real warmth in her smile. Coming forward, she stood beside the bed, looking down at him.

'How are you feeling now, Frank?' she asked, and there was something personal in her voice.

'Hungry,' he answered, 'and a little confused. What happened? How long have I been lying here?'

She said: 'To answer your first question, you got a bullet in the arm when you killed Rand in the barn. You've been unconscious for almost two days, delirious most of the time, always muttering under your breath, none of it making any sense.'

Frank sighed. He shook his head. 'Two days,' he murmured. 'That's a long time to be unconscious just because of a slug. They got it out, I suppose?'

'Yes, we got Doc Farrow in from town. He said it was the combined effect of the bullet and the burns you got which caused your condition. You'll be on your feet in a week or so if you lie here quietly and follow orders. If you don't, then he'll wash his hands of you.

I'm to see to it that you do as you're told.'

'And the rest of Klagge's men?' he inquired.

'They lost twelve men in the gunfight. When they failed in their attempt to burn us out, they tried to rush us, only to be caught in a crossfire from the house and the bunkhouse. They pulled out and headed back to town.'

'I suppose it's too much to hope that Klagge and Laredo were among the dead?'

She nodded. 'They're both still alive, probably still plotting against us. But we're ready for them now.'

'He can still bring in plenty of hired killers. Provided he pays a high enough price, he can get them from all over the territory.'

'Maybe so. But once the hill people heard about Clark's murder, they realized where they stand now. We can draw twenty or thirty of them to us any time we wish. Klagge knows this and he's treading carefully right now, not quite as sure of himself as he was.'

'I hope you're right. He's not the sort of man to let one setback put him off his stride.'

Stella nodded. She looked at him for a long moment in her searching way, then turned. 'I'll get you something to eat. You've had scarcely anything at all these past two days.'

Frank lay back on the bed, thinking back to the old days for a moment, the good feeling, with its promises, its memories, the starlight shimmering faintly over a trail whose end he did not know, came back to him. But it did not linger. After it, the more recent recollections came crowding in on it, forcing it away, leaving him with only the nagging emptiness of mind and the dull ache of the pain in his shoulder.

* * *

Leaving the hotel, Austen Klagge went out into the night's blackness that lay thick and heavy over Fresno City, leaning his body into the wind that howled along the main street, hurrying the grey dust from one end of the town to the other. There was still a tremendous heat in the air, but all afternoon he had seen the great thunderheads rising up on the north-western horizon and knew that they betokened a storm brewing out over the mountains. As he made his way across the street, shielding his face against the stinging clouds of dust, the first great, hissing flare of lightning lashed across the heavens, sparking through the piled up tumult of the boiling clouds, and for the space of a fraction of a second the whole world was lit up as bright as day, with every detail around him imprinting itself on his retina. Then, close on its heels, the utter blackness closed in and, as if a mighty curtain had closed on the whole of creation, the thunder smashed and roared against his eardrums.

There was a yellow glow showing

through the street window of Fent Corday's office, the flickering light of a lamp, the flame rising and falling as the wind caught it. He rapped loudly on the door, waited as the gusting air snatched the breath from his lips and tore at him as it whistled along the street. More lightning ripped across the heavens and the first heavy drops of rain were beginning to fall, beating against the roofs of the buildings, as the door was unlocked. The lawyer pushed his face around the edge of the door, saw who it was standing there and unlatched the chain, opening the door fully to let Klagge in.

'Is Laredo here?' Klagge asked harshly as the other leaned his weight against the door to close it in the face of the wind.

'Came five minutes ago. Said you'd be along.' Corday ushered him into the front office.

Klagge gave Laredo a brief nod as he went inside, sank down into the chair at the table, taking off his hat and laying it down in front of him.

'Those men of yours, Laredo,' Klagge said, when they were all settled. 'I see some of them are arriving in town.'

The other gave a brief nod. 'Half a dozen put up at the hotel an hour ago. There'll be the same number ridin' in tomorrow or the day after. You plannin' to make another night raid on Michener?'

'I'm tryin' to make up my mind about it.' Klagge took out a cigar, bit the end off it, then struck a match and applied the flame to it, his cheeks sucking in for several moments until he had it going. 'Right now, though, I'm not so sure it would work any better than it did the last time.'

'But with these twelve men, we could overrun that place in an hour,' said Laredo.

'I'm not so convinced about that.' Klagge shook his head. 'You may not have heard, but most of the hill folk have thrown in their lot with Michener since Forrester was killed. I guess I ought to have foreseen that possibility but at the time it seemed a good idea to get him out of the way after he was warnin' Michener every time we rode against the Lazy T.'

Laredo, twisting up a cigarette, lit it and peered closely through the smoke, staring at Klagge with narrowed eyes. 'Then you've got some other idea?'

'Could be. Seems to me that as far as Kent Michener is concerned, we've been concentratin' our attentions on the wrong person.'

'You mean Corrie?' put in Corday.

'That's right. I had him figured for a dangerous man. I still do. But from what I hear, Kent Michener was prepared to leave him to hang when we had him on that trumped-up murder charge. It was the girl who took things into her own hands and brought those men out to stop the hangin'.'

'So? We're still got Corrie to contend with.'

Klagge leaned back. He said softly: 'The trouble with you, Fent, is that you're so tangled with points of law that you fail to understand human thoughts and emotions. That ranch means a lot to Michener. Even if I was to offer him a very fair price for it, he would never sell. He's built himself a little empire here, with his own sweat and toil, and that means everything to a man. But there's somethin' — or someone — else who means more to him than the ranch.'

Corday's eyes widened a little as he found the meaning behind the other's words. 'You mean his daughter, of course.'

'Exactly. Now if we had her in our hands, we could really force him out. Nothin' could be simpler.'

Corday rubbed his chin musingly. After a while, he said, gravely: 'Always admitting that you did manage to kidnap her, where would you take her to be sure they wouldn't find her before you'd forced him to sign the place over to you?'

'I've been thinkin' about that. Seems

to me there's only one place. The Silver Lode mine.'

'Hewitt's place?'

'Sure. Only he won't know anythin' about it. I've been makin' a few discreet inquiries around town. Seems they aren't workin' the vein right now. Hewitt has sent samples of ore from a fresh seam to the assay office in Fort Arthur. He won't get any answer back for more'n a week. In that time we can do all we need to do before he can butt in.'

'And if Michener doesn't come through, even though you have the girl? If Corrie and the other start snoopin' around and get a little too close to home?' asked Laredo.

Klagge's smile was a frozen, vicious thing in the lamplight. 'Then there's always the dynamite they keep down there. If Corrie or any of the others get too close and start probin' around in there, an accident can always be arranged.'

The grey light of an early dawn was seeping in through the windows when Frank woke. He felt warm and strangely refreshed, although at times, during the night, booming echoes of sound had penetrated through the dulling layers of sleep to reach him, as the storm had crashed and rolled about the ranch, the thunder hammering back and forth between the hills, echoing and re-echoing along the valley. He heard it dimly, as he would have heard sounds in a dream and then, towards dawn, it had faded out and when he woke he could recall little of it.

With an effort, he pushed his shoulders up on to the pillow, stared out through the window. He could just make out the courtyard and part of the corral and he saw at once that the storm of the night had broken in its full fury over the valley. The dust was now mud and although the rain had stopped, he guessed that plenty had fallen through the dark hours. But unless more came, it would not mean an end to the drought, only a brief alleviation. If the sun came out, bringing with it the punishing heat that lay like a muffling blanket over the land, it would suck up all this moisture within a few hours, leaving the ground as hard and caked as before. Then the hot, drying winds would turn it all back into dust once more.

How long he lay there he wasn't sure. But eventually he heard sounds coming from the direction of the kitchen, smelled frying bacon and potatoes overlaid with hot coffee, bringing a pang of hunger pain to the corners of his mouth. The door of the room opened five minutes later and Stella Michener came in, carrying a tray which she set down on the bed in front of him.

'Better eat up. The doctor's orders were you were to have nourishing food and I was to see that you ate it.'

'I feel hungry enough to eat a horse,' he murmured.

'That's a good sign.' He heard her let out a small sigh as she stepped back, still watching him. After a pause, she said: 'Why did you ever ride into this territory in the first place, Frank? Looking for someone, or running away from something?'

'A man always seems to be doin' one or the other,' he replied.

'That's not really an answer,' she said gravely. She waited patiently, then when he did not reply, shrugged and went over to the window, looking down on the courtyard. 'I'll be riding into town today. We need further supplies and — '

'Are you sure it's safe for you to go? Klagge hasn't given up, you know. He's still bitter about the way you rescued me from the end of that rope.'

She showed him a lift of her chin and made an almost imperious gesture with her right hand. 'I'll be quite safe there, even from Klagge.'

Frank gave her a bright-sharp stare.

'You seem very self-confident. I hope you're not under-estimatin' Klagge. Somehow, I get the impression he cares very little for chivalry.'

Stella's lips drew back from her teeth in a smile. 'Nothing will happen to me, but it's good to have your concern.'

The day had been long and hot, with the sun drawing the moisture from the ground, baking it to a hard consistency. The small streams that had been formed during the night when the storm had lashed the territory were already drying up fast and would soon have disappeared altogether. Now, however, on the way back from town, the afternoon sun was sending the cooling shadows of the hills down across the winding trail and the earlier breeze that had brought the dust gusting in eddies over the buck-board had died and a fresher, cooler wind had sprung up, moving the lower branches of the pines on the brows of the hills.

Stella Michener sat on the tongue of the buckboard, watching the shadows lengthen about her. Despite the cooling, revitalizing effect of the breeze against her face and body, she was frowning to herself and scarcely aware of her surroundings. In town she had learned some disturbing news. The storekeepers had all commented on the large number of strangers who had ridden into town the previous day, putting up at the hotel and then seen later in deep conversation with Laredo Ford and Austen Klagge. There was general speculation that these were more hired gunmen brought in from the border country to replace those that Klagge had lost in his abortive attempt to take the Lazy T ranch and that, with his numbers swollen by these fresh men, he would find far less difficulty in finishing the job if he took it into his head to attack again.

For the first few miles out of town she had driven the horses to the point of exhaustion. Now she had realized her mistake and was allowing them to take their own time. The sound of a shot jerked her out of her reverie. Swiftly she turned her head, eyes searching the brush to either side for any tell-tale sign of smoke, but saw nothing. Puzzled, her mind raced ahead. It could have been some rider shooting at game, there was plenty in this area. On the other hand, it could be something a little more ominous. Frank Corrie's warning came back to her and the silence which ensued after the slowly atrophying echoes of the gunshot had died away pressed oppressively down on her.

Acting on impulse, she jerked up the whip, laid it over the backs of the horses. Dispiritedly, for they were still exhausted from the long run in the full heat of the day, they increased their gait.

Less than thirty seconds after the first shot another sounded. This time she distinctly heard the faint flicker of sound and the slug struck the upright beside her arm, chipping a sliver out of it, leaving a ragged white mark in the wood.

One of the horses reared and plunged, pawing at the air, almost dragging itself free of the traces. Desperately Stella held on to the reins, struggling to calm the terrified animal. Ahead of her the trail looked deserted and she had already guessed, from the side where the bullet had struck, that the shot had come from behind her, from somewhere on the right.

Uttering a loud shout, she used the whip once more, for the last time, giving the horses their head. The buck-board rolled forward at an increasing pace, jolting and swaying as the wheels hit the upthrusting rocks which poked themselves up from the dust of the trail. There was the sound of pounding hoofs behind her. Throwing a quick glance over her shoulder, she saw the two men riding down from the rough ground less than three hundred yards away, kicking their horses' flanks as they moved towards the trail.

More shots came after her as the two men swung down on to the trail and took up the pursuit. Soon, however, it was obvious that they were not aiming at her, but at the horses. It was then that a chill of fear settled over her. The men wanted her alive, for what purpose she could not yet imagine.

Clinging desperately to the side of the buckboard with one hand, holding on to the reins with the other, she fought to guide the panicked horses along the twisting trail, knowing that one wrong move by either of the animals could mean the end. She was too much a realist to know that she could not hope to outrun the men behind her. Their horses had probably been rested most of the day while they had lain in wait for her and a man on horseback could always ride faster than a buckboard; but at the back of her mind, overriding every other consideration, was the illogical feeling that although she was still several miles from the Lazy T ranch, the nearer she got to it before they caught up with her, the better the chances of some of her father's hands coming on the scene.

Slowly, inevitably, the gap between the swaying buckboard and the two riders diminished. The end came swiftly, almost too swiftly for Stella to comprehend. As they swung around a bend in the trail a slug tore into the arched neck of one of the horses. The mortally wounded animal plunged sideways, twisting in the traces, going down on to its knees. Before the girl could do anything to save herself, the buckboard tilted crazily, seemed to leap high into the air, wheels spinning uselessly, before crashing down on to the brush-covered ground, overturning as it did so. There was the rending crash of wood splintering as it smashed on to the rocks. Thrown clear by the impact, Stella hit the hard earth with a jolt which hammered all of the breath from her body. Red lights burst behind her eyes as her head crashed against the ground and she had a brief vision of the buckboard, battered almost beyond recognition, being dragged through the dust by the remaining horse. Then a thin curtain of shimmering haze descended over her vision. Through the roaring in her head she heard the beat of hoofs close by and the shouts of men.

Sobbing for breath, struggling to hold on to her buckling consciousness, Stella pulled herself to her feet. As she saw the two men swing down from their saddles and move towards her, she went for the small handgun she always carried at her waist. Grinning, Laredo Ford strode forward, grabbed at her wrist before she could bring up the gun to cover him. His fingers bit into her flesh with a steely grip, squeezing hard until she was forced to drop the gun, sobbing in frustrated anger.

'Why didn't you shoot me in the back as you always do with your victims?' she challenged wildly, trembling, more angry than afraid.

Laredo grabbed her shoulders, his leering face pushed close to hers. Acting on instinct, Stella drew her clawed hand across his face. With a wild cry of pain, Laredo jerked his head back, eyes blazing, his fingers going up to his cheek where the twin streaks of blood were beginning to ooze along his flesh. 'Why — you damned she-cat,' he hissed fiercely. 'I ought to have shot you for that like you said.' He was breathing heavily, lips twisted into a vicious snarl and, for the first time, Stella felt fear bite through her mind. She recognized that here was a man who would stop at nothing, who held human life cheap, man or woman. He slapped her hand aside, swore bitterly, and drew back his clenched fist, ready to drive it into her face.

'Careful, Laredo.' The second man's voice was a warning. 'Remember what Klagge said. We were not to harm her. He'll be mighty angry if he finds she's been mauled.'

Laredo swung on the other. 'Shut up!' he snarled harshly. 'I know what I'm doin'. If Klagge asks questions, she always got hurt when the buckboard went over on to its side.'

'She's likely to talk,' the other pointed out. He glanced up at the lowering sun. 'Besides, we'd better get away from here. No tellin' who might happen along and we want her out of sight before dark.'

'Where are you takin' me?' Stella asked hoarsely. She tried to keep her voice from shaking.

'You'll find that out in good time.' Laredo turned to his companion. 'Get that horse out of the traces and bring it over here.'

The other went over to the wrecked buckboard, glanced at the dead horse, then unfastened the traces from the other, and led it forward. 'What do we do for a saddle?'

'You ride that one,' Laredo said. 'The girl will ride yours.'

The other grumbled a little under his breath as he swung up on to the horse's back, but made no objection. Laredo swung on Stella. 'All right,' he snapped. The marks on his face where her fingernails had clawed him gave him a terrifying appearance. 'Mount up. Don't give us any trouble and you'll be all right. Try anything and I'll forget what Klagge said.' His tone was menacing.

Stella twisted her lips bitterly. 'I might have known that Klagge would be at the back of something like this. If he thinks he can get away with it, he's a fool. Frank Corrie will know how to deal with him — and you two men also.'

Laredo shook his head. 'Reckon that Corrie just got lucky with Jose. The next time it'll be the finish for him.'

Laredo's face took on an ugly look. Savagely, he motioned the girl towards the waiting horse, paused while she mounted, then climbed easily into the saddle, jerked his mount's head around and rode towards the wrecked buckboard, taking a large sheet of paper from his pocket as he did so. He left it on the splintered seat where it would be plainly visible. Then he touched spurs to his horse's flanks and led the way out across the rough country of the mesa, away from the main trail, the girl following and Munford bringing up the rear.

Stella's body was a mass of pain when dusk came. The bruising she had received when she had been thrown from the buckboard had left her limbs throbbing fercely, and the long ride across the mesa, with the breeze blowing the sand continually into her face, and the glare of the setting sun flaring in her eyes, made things even worse. At first she had had no idea of where they were headed. She judged that they were swinging in a wide circle to the west of Fresno City, and had thought, initially, that they were perhaps taking her back to town by a circuitous route. But that thought had died a little while before when Laredo had turned west again, heading towards the high hills that stood out in deep purple shadow on the horizon.

She had always known that Laredo

Ford was a cold-blooded killer, but before she had considered him as no different from many of the outlaws who infested the hills around town. Men who had killed and were on the run from the law, hiding out from everyone. But now that she had seen him at close quarters, seen the way he acted, she felt both contempt and fear for the man. She told herself that at the moment he was merely obeying orders given him by Austen Klagge, but she didn't doubt that, given the chance, he would murder her cold-bloodedly and without a single twinge of conscience. That paper he had left on the smashed buckboard. Even though she had not seen it, she could guess what it had been. A note left for anyone who found it — and someone would find it once she failed to turn up at the ranch before dark — telling her father that if he ever wanted to see her alive, he would have to do exactly as Klagge said. She was to be the hostage to force her father's hand. A faint feeling of despair went through her mind and she temporarily forgot her own aches and pains. Her father would have no choice now. Gunmen he could face; but the possibility that he might never see her again would force his hand where everything else had failed. If only she had listened to Frank. But she had been so determined and headstrong, so sure that nothing would happen to her that she had ridden into danger with her eyes shut. Now she — and her father — would have to pay the price of her folly.

'How much further do we have to go?' she asked, forcing the words through parched and cracked lips.

Laredo said nothing, did not even give any indication that he had heard her. It was the man riding behind her who answered. 'Not far now. Just over to the hills.'

She wrinkled her brows in thought. She knew most of this country and the range of hills that lay directly ahead did not provide any hiding places and, as far as she knew, no one lived there. The only place of any importance was the Silver Lode mine, and it seemed out of the question that they would be taking her there. She recalled that Cy Hewitt, the owner of the mine, had been present among those in the square when they had tried to hang Frank, but she did not believe he would have any hand in this. But on the face of it, there seemed no other explanation. Had she misjudged Hewitt? Was he in with Klagge, working with him to take over the entire territory?

An hour later her doubts were resolved as they entered the narrow pass which led up to the entrance of the Silver Lode mine. The sun had gone down behind the hills fifteen minutes earlier and the land lay in deep blue shadow, with the coolness of air flowing down the hills in their faces. Her eyes moved across the open area where the sides of the canyon sloped down to the trail, up to where the mine works showed darkly in the sandstone escarpment high above them.

They put their tired horses to the steep shale-covered slope. It was hard going. The deep shadows hid obstacles along the track and they had to pick their way cautiously among the boulders strewn in irregular profusion all about them. Presently they drew level with the cyanide vats built where there was a small stretch of level ground between two slopes. Furrowed piles of gravel stood humped on either side and fifty yards beyond the cyanide vats, cradled in their wooden baskets, were the company buildings with the steel rails leading directly into the gaping hole in the side of the hill.

Laredo reined up his mount on the flat stretch of ground, looked about him approvingly. 'Reckon Klagge was right about the place,' he murmured. 'From here a couple of men could hold off an army. We can spot anybody comin' along this trail at the bottom of the slope and pick 'em off from the mine buildings before they get near us.'

The other man glanced up at the great wall of red sand-stone that loomed in front of them, blocking off the other end of the narrow trail. 'Reckon it will be impossible for anybody to reach us *that* way,' he said significantly.

'You're damned right,' growled Laredo. 'So there's only one way up and we can watch every inch of it.'

'What if they decide to hit us durin' the night?'

'What makes you think they'll ever look here?'

The other shrugged. 'Just wantin' to take every possible precaution,' he retorted.

'Then if that's the case, you can hole up in one of the shacks yonder and keep watch.' He grinned as he prodded his mount forward. 'Reckon if you fall asleep and they do come, you'll be the first to get a bullet.'

8

Hard Justice

Gritting his teeth against the pain that jarred occasionally through his shoulder, Frank Corrie stared down at the wrecked buckboard, lying crushed on its side against a short stretch of bare, weathered rock, one shattered wheel on top of it. The dead horse lay a short distance away, feet still tangled in the leather traces.

Kent Michener, his features white and drawn, stood beside the wreck, the sheet of paper held in his right hand. His lips were moving as he read it through for the tenth time, but no sound came out. Anger and fear and frustration were strong inside him, each battling for supremacy in his mind. Finally he looked up at where Frank sat forward in the saddle.

'What do I do, Frank?' His voice was little more than a husky whisper. 'I can't allow them to kill her. She's all I have left since her mother died. I have to do as Klagge says.'

'We could always grab Klagge and force him to talk,' said one of the men nearby. 'Reckon if we threatened him with a bullet, he might tell us where he's got her holed up.'

'That won't work,' Frank pointed out 'He'd make damned sure we didn't find her alive if we tried that stunt.'

'So I've got no choice,' Michener said bitterly. 'If it's the spread against Stella's life, then he can have everything, damn his soul to hell.'

Frank said nothing. In the dimness of late dusk it was difficult to make out details, but bending low in the saddle, he could see where the second horse that had been taken out of the traces had left its tracks, leading to a spot a few yards distant. Gently he gigged his mount over. There were fresh marks visible in the sand. Two other horses, he guessed, although it was not possible to be absolutely certain because of the confused nature of the sign. The trail, he noticed, led west, out across the wide stretch of the mesa. For a man who had any tracking ability at all, it might not be too difficult to follow that sign, especially since the riders did not seem to have gone to any pains to erase it.

Going back to Michener, he said slowly: 'They took off in that direction. Kent. Either they were headed back into town, moving around from the west so they wouldn't be seen, or they're heading towards the hills.'

Kent Michener eyed him dully for a moment, then dragged his thoughts back to the present with an effort. 'That doesn't help us,' he said tautly. 'There must be a hundred places in town where they could be keepin' her. And as for the hills, ain't no place out there where they could be takin' her.'

'Maybe not.' Frank reached a sudden decision. 'But I'd like a couple of men to ride with me, to follow their trail. We might be able to catch up with them before we know it, and if we could take 'em by surprise — '

Michener pondered that for a long, speculative moment. The intensity of his thoughts showed clearly on his lined features. Suddenly he seemed to have aged ten years.

'You know it's Stella's life you're gamblin' with, Frank.'

'I know. Believe me, I realize that just as much as you do.'

'And you won't take any unnecessary chances?'

'No,' Frank said.

'Then take any of my men you like. They're all good men and — '

'I'll come, Frank.' Duprey spoke up from the other side of the smashed buckboard. 'You owe it to George and me to take us along. We've both got a score to settle with Klagge and Ford.'

Frank gave the other a piercing glance. What the ex-sheriff said was true enough. Of all the men there, with the exception perhaps of Michener himself, these two men had the most to settle with Klagge. But there was the distinct possibility that this could prove to be a tremendous disadvantage under these conditions. They might tend to act rashly when they came within shooting distance of these kidnappers, instead of acting with caution and patience. Still —

He gave a brief nod. 'All right,' he agreed. 'Saddle up and we'll move out before it gets any darker.'

★   ★   ★

It was dark as the three men rode out into the wide vastness of the mesa, with stars showing point by point in the inverted vault of the Heavens. After an hour the moon rose, flooding the scene with a pale, cold light, giving them enough radiance to see by. They rode in silence, each man engrossed in his own thoughts. In the lead, Frank paused every now and again to check the ground. The trail was becoming rougher as they swung around in a wide circle. West was five miles of open country before one reached the low range of hills. South-east lay Fresno City. As yet there was no indication of which way the trail would eventually lead them. The possibility that it would swing south and head in the direction of the Mexico border was there, but very remote. Klagge would realize that so long as he held Stella Michener as his bargaining piece, she would have to be kept well hidden but close by, if he was to force her father's hand.

It was necessarily slow progress. Now and then they lost the trail where it had been obliterated by the rain, and then they were forced to scout around in an ever-widening circle until they picked it up again. Frank sat slouched forward in the saddle, with his hat brim over his head. He could have been asleep, judging by the loose, easy way his body followed the swaying motions of the black bay, but he was, in fact, wide awake and his eyes missed nothing. He was bone tired and the pain in his shoulder was now a dull, diffuse ache that was even worse than the stabbing pangs of agony which had preceded it. But he stayed in the saddle and followed the tell-tale sign of hoofs in the sand because this was nothing new as far as he was concerned. He had stood many night watches over a herd of cattle and then stayed upright in the saddle throughout the whole of the following day. This was all part of a rider's job.

As the moon climbed higher into the clear sky, it was easier to pick out the tracks. In most places the sand had been swept smooth by the wind of the previous morning and the trail stood out clearly. In spite of this, he was a trifle worried. Why had these men been so confident that they had made no attempt to hide their trail? Did they believe that the chances of being followed were so remote that there wasn't any necessity for them to go to all of that trouble? Or had they done this deliberately, hoping to lure someone into tracking them down? It was this last possibility that began preying on his thoughts. He took to lifting his head, almost standing upright in the saddle, peering ahead into the deep night stillness, eyes alert and watchful, ready to pick out any sign of trouble up ahead. But always he saw nothing.

Shortly before midnight they reached the point where the trail turned abruptly. Frank reined up his mount and peered closely at the tracks.

'What is it?' murmured Duprey. 'Somethin' wrong?'

'I'm not sure.' Frank pointed with his good arm. 'They headed in that direction, due west.'

Duprey rubbed his chin, fingers scraping on the day's growth of stubble. 'Nothin' there,' he said musingly. 'Why'd they head that way?'

'Reckon they might be tryin' to throw us off the trail?' inquired George.

'It's possible, though judgin' by the

way they've left their trail plain for anyone to see, it doesn't make sense.'

Frank probed the moonlit terrain with his glance. 'What lies in that direction?' he asked.

Duprey shrugged his shoulders. 'Once you get over the hills it goes clear to the California border with nothin' in between.'

'Any place in the hills where they could hole up?'

'Not that I know of, unless — ' He paused.

'Unless what?'

'There's only the Silver Lode mine,' Duprey answered. 'But they wouldn't hole up there. Hewitt isn't on such friendly terms with Klagge as all that.'

'Aren't you forgetin' that the mine isn't bein' worked now?' broke in George quickly. 'Hewitt is waitin' for that assay report from Fort Arthur. The place will be deserted right now.'

'Hell, you're right. It's the very place they would head for. Once they're holed up there, it would take an army to get them out. They can watch the trail up to the mine for the best part of a mile, cover every inch of it with rifle fire.'

Frank lifted his canteen, tilted it to his lips and let the cool water trickle down his throat. So that was the reason these men had not bothered to cover their tracks. Even if they were followed, they would consider themselves to be quite safe.

'You know the lay-out of this place?'

'I do,' George said. 'Worked there for a while before I took on the deputy's job in town. Like Clem says, it's almost impregnable. Only one way up to it, along a narrow trail leading up the side of the hill. There are the big crushers and cyanide vats half-way up the slope on a level stretch of ground, and most of the mine buildings are there too. Just about impossible to go in down the side of the trail, and it comes to a stop at the top where it leads right down into the mine itself.'

'No way over the top?'

'Not a chance.' The other's tone was decisive. 'Even if you managed to get up to the top of the bluffs, it's a sheer drop down to the mine entrance. Not a handhold in sight.'

'So we'd have to go up from the front.' Frank wiped away the sweat from his forehead where the rim of his hat had left a red mark in the flesh.

'That's right. And with there bein' two of 'em, there will be one always on watch while the other keeps an eye on the girl.'

'Then our only chance is to hit them during the night,' he said. 'Let's go.' He led the way across a sage-dotted saucer of land, climbing the long saddle of ground that lay beyond.

Two hours later, with the moon temporarily blotted out by a long layer of thick cloud, they came within sight of the narrow trail that led up into the side of the hills. Frank could see where the trail narrowed swiftly as it led up to where the dark shadows of the wooden shacks halfway up the slope showed in the dimness against the lighter background of the sandstone. On either side they could see the gigantic rock formations close to the trail and, dominating everything, the great sandstone bluff which rose sheer above the mine workings. It was easy to see that George had been right in his assessment of the position. Once more Frank was thankful to the fate which had prompted him to bring the other along. If anyone could help now, he could, knowing this place intimately.

Narrowing his eyes, he took in every detail of the situation. He reckoned it most likely that the girl was inside the workings themselves, with one of the men, the other on guard near the huge vats or inside one of the shacks. They angled their mounts to the right, reining up in the shadow of the stunted trees that grew on the edge of the mesa where it met the foothills, out of sight of the mine trail.

'We go the rest of the way on foot,'

he murmured softly, pulling the Winchester from its scabbard, checking that it was loaded. 'And no noise now.'

George pointed off into the trees. 'There's a small trail there,' he said. 'It's nothin' more'n a game track, and it only comes out thirty yards or so below the vats. But it should help us to get close to them without being seen. My guess is they don't know of it and they'll be watching the main track.'

Frank nodded, agreeing. They moved the horses into the brush, tethered them to one of the trees, and moved in on foot, climbing into the tumbled rocks. There was no sound as they edged forward and Frank could feel the tightness inside him growing more pronounced. His shoulders were pulled up, tensed and every faint sound as their boots scraped the bare, exposed rock, or their clothing rasped against the crackly bushes that grew in dense profusion on either side, sounded unnaturally loud in the taut, tense stillness.

It was only in his imagination that the sound seemed to carry so far, he told himself. Still he could feel the tightness in him, and the thought did not help him to relax.

They moved steadily through the brush patch, stopping when they came to the end of it, pausing a while before Frank ventured out into the open rocks. It was ten minutes before he came upon the spot where the tracks angled up from below. To his right he could just make out the squat shapes of the vats balanced in their wooden cradles. Beyond them were the shacks, clustered in two groups on either side of the trail. He crouched down and waited for a moment until his eyes grew accustomed to the gloom.

He was debating: only one man would be on guard if they had the girl somewhere inside the mine itself. If that were so, his best spot would be in one of the shacks, stationed near a window, and he could be either on the same side of the track or on the other. There was no way of telling. Hunched back on his heels, he knew he could either wait in the hope that the other would make a move — or he could go hunting, leaving these two men to cover his rear.

With Stella in the hands of these men, it was not in him to wait. Turning, he motioned to the others to move up.

'I figure one of them is holed up in one of the shacks. They wouldn't leave the way up unguarded. The question is, which one is he in?'

'No way of saying,' murmured Duprey. 'You figure we could circle around 'em and — '

He broke off as Frank caught his arm in a tight grip. There was no need for him to say anything. They had all seen it. There were three shacks on the far side, forty yards or so from where they lay. In the centre one a faint glow showed briefly in one of the windows, like the low, orange burning of a cigarette tip. Frank stared at it steadily until he was sure of it. The window, he observed, commanded the whole length of the trail leading up the hillside. From that position, crouched against the window ledge, a man might see many angles he could not see from any of the other buildings. Whoever it was up there watching the trail, he had chosen his place well.

'Stay here,' he whispered. 'He's in there for sure.'

'We could circle around and take him from three sides,' said George.

'No. We can't afford any gunplay. This has got to be done silently. Once that other *hombre* is warned, Stella is finished.' He laid the Winchester down against the rocks, unbuckled his gun-belt, and slid the knife from its sheath, testing the edge momentarily with the ball of his thumb. Then he backed away from the trail's edge and retreated into the deeper shadows. Even as he slid among the rocks, the moon broke free from the clouds and sailed majestically into the clear sky, throwing light and shadow over the rugged terrain. Frank cursed softly under his breath. He squinted up at the sky, saw there was no chance of the moon going in again, and kept moving forward. He crossed the open stretch of the trail twenty yards above the cluster of shacks and circled behind the buildings on the far side, padding forward as noiselessly as a cat.

When he reached the rear of the centre building he spotted a doorway and moved towards it, pausing to listen tensely before pushing it gently open and stepping inside. In the pale glow of the moonlight filtering in through the dusty window, he made out the packing cases scattered over the floor of the room, and guessed this was some kind of store. There was the musty smell of a place not often used, and he could smell the dust dragged up by his feet, stinging the back of his nostrils.

There was another door set in the wall facing him, its blackness less than that of the wall. Something scurried across the beaten earth of the floor, ran into the corner and paused for a moment, red eyes glaring at him from the dimness, before the rat vanished. That was the only sound. Yet he knew that somewhere just beyond the door a man lay in wait for him, watching the trail for any sign of movement, his finger on the trigger of his weapon.

Carefully he set down one foot in front of the other, testing the hummocky surface of the floor, edging around the packing cases. He let his weight fall slow and easy in the stillness, holding his breath until it hurt in his lungs. Reaching the half-open door, he realized that his fingers were gripping the haft of the knife so tightly they were almost numb as the blood eased out of them. With an effort, he forced himself to relax his grip.

Still no noise from inside the other room, but some kind of coolness seemed to reach out of the shadows around him and ruffle the small hairs on the back of his neck. He paused, still uncertain of the other man's whereabouts. Then, superimposed on the quiet, he heard a man breathing and, a moment later, a sudden scrape of sound that he identified as a booted heel twisting on the floor as the other crushed out the butt of his cigarette.

He stopped and stood fast, listening into the fathomless blackness that faced him, peering in through the crack in the half-open door. Gradually he was able to make out the pale square of the window and the head and shoulders of the gunman etched against it. Very slowly he lifted the knife. This had to be done swiftly and silently. He took a step forward, edged into the room. Still the other had heard nothing, did not turn his head.

Then, as if some instinctive warning had penetrated his mind, the man suddenly turned sharply. Frank saw his mouth jerk open in stunned surprise, saw him swing away from the window, hauling the rifle round in a single, fluid movement. Swiftly, Frank swung his arm. The knife flew in a faint flash of silver across the room, embedded itself in the other's throat. The man uttered a strangled gasp as he fell back. For a moment he retained his grip on the rifle, then it slipped from his nerveless fingers and clattered dully on the floor.

The man's body twisted against the rickety window frame as he hung there for what seemed an interminable time. His eyes, wide and full of a surprise beyond life, stared at Frank, but already they were beginning to glaze over, to lose their brightness.

'Goddamn you, Corrie,' he mumbled. He tried to say something further but at that moment a rush of blood flooded from his mouth and the strings which had held him up snapped and he slid inertly to the floor, arms and legs splayed out on the dirt. Frank listened and heard no breathing, went forward cautiously. Withdrawing the knife, he wiped it on the man's shirt, and thrust it back into his belt. His foot touched the other's body and he bent over the man, shaking his arm for a moment, feeling the lumped looseness fall back as he released his hold.

Getting to his feet, he went back through the building, out at the rear and retraced his steps until he came upon the two men crouched in the lee of the rocks.

'Did you find him?' Duprey asked.

Frank nodded. 'He's dead,' he said quietly. 'That's one chore finished. But we still have to find that other killer.'

'You think he's in the mine yonder?'

'Sure of it. That *hombre* was alone, watchin' the trail. I doubt if the other will be in any of the buildings.'

His eyes roamed over the deserted buildings, dark in the flooding moonlight. 'It could be,' he said slowly, 'that the other man figures he's safe so long as he reckons his partner is down here keepin' watch. Wouldn't be any sense in them both stayin' awake all night.'

'So you think we stand a chance of gettin' up there without bein' spotted?'

'I reckon it's a calculated risk. One we'll have to take if we're to do anythin' at all.'

They moved out into the open, kept

their eyes on the gaping black mouth of the mine entrance, where the palely gleaming steel rails vanished into oblivion into the face of the mountain. Going up slowly in the treacherously shifting sand underfoot, picking their way cautiously, they moved along the side of the trail, sticking to the moon-thrown shadows wherever possible. No sound came from the mine and, better still, none came from either the cyanide vats or the other buildings.

Ten yards from the entrance, Frank motioned them to halt. 'We go in here in single file with a short distance between us,' he said. 'This time, if anybody spots this other *hombre* and can get a clear shot at him without endangering the girl, he does so without waitin'. Got that?'

The two men nodded. All three knew that it might be the only chance they would get, and that Stella Michener's life hung in the balance. If the dice fell against them, the second kidnapper would put a bullet into her before they could get off a single shot at him. Even a speeding bullet was not quicker than the reflex action of a man's hand on the trigger of a gun. All three men were acutely aware of this as they moved into the midnight blackness inside the tunnel of the mine.

Now they were all three forced to move forward by sense of touch. There was not even a spark of light inside the tunnel once they had moved only a few feet inside the entrance. Looking back over his shoulder, Frank was just able to make out the figures of the two men, hugging the out-thrusting rocks, picking their way along the edge of the rails, their silhouettes just seen against the pale opening behind them. Then he turned his attention to the blackness in front of him, deep and impenetrable, with nothing to relieve it. It kept going through his mind. Where would the other kidnapper hole up? Who was it and what had they already done to Stella?

The thought of any hurt coming to

her was a consuming flame inside his mind, almost breaking him in half. Previously he had always considered himself as above being hurt by other people. Now, almost without him wanting it to happen, he knew that a slender girl had, in spite of everything, become the most important thing in the world to him. He wondered briefly if Kent Michener had realized this when he had sent him after her.

His fingers touched an outjutting rock and he edged carefully around it, sliding his feet forward. Rocks lay everywhere on the floor of the mine; and in this intense blackness that lay like a piece of velvet thrust against his eyes, so thick that he could almost feel it, it would be easy to kick something and send echoes rattling along the whole length of the tunnel.

As he stood with his body pressed tightly against the cold, moisture-running wall, he realized with a start that the blackness ahead of him was not quite as absolute as it had been only a few moments before. He narrowed his eyes as he veered into the tunnel, unsure whether or not he was imagining it. Then he realized he could see the shape of the rocks against a pale glow that came from around a corner in the tunnel and, as he took a step forward, the sound of muted voices reached him.

Sucking in a long, heavy gust of air, he let it come out through his nostrils in slow pinches. He stood rigid. It was Laredo Ford's voice. He felt certain of it. As he waited, it came again, tight and angry.

'Your old man had better come up with that ranch,' Laredo was saying. 'Because if he don't, Klagge will let me deal with you — and I figure you can guess what that would mean.'

'I think that, without doubt, you are the lowest and most contemptible creature it has ever been my misfortune to come across.' Stella's voice was so low and intense that it was almost a whisper, yet the words carried clearly to where Frank crouched against the rocks. 'As soon as Frank Corrie catches up with you, and he will, mark my words, it'll mean the end of all your evil life.'

Laredo uttered a harsh laugh. 'Corrie will never find us here, and even if he did, he'd never get to the mine alive. There's a rifle down the slope waitin' for any man who puts in an appearance.'

'You think that will stop him?' There was contempt in the girl's voice now. 'He isn't the kind of man who shoots men down when they are unarmed and have no chance to defend themselves.'

'Fernandez had it coming,' snarled the other. 'I always remember those who look down on me, and that lousy Mex had it coming for years. He seemed to think he was better than me.'

'So you shot him down in cold blood and then tried to pin his murder on Frank. And Corday was in on it too. He lied his way to that rigged jury so as to get in with Klagge.'

'Sure. Why not? Klagge is going to be

the big man in this territory very soon. And he remembers those who help him.' There was a pause, then Laredo said thinly: 'But as for you and me. I figure this is the time to tame you. You're another one of those who thinks she's so goddamn high and mighty that men like me are nothin' more than dirt under your feet. You need to be taught a lesson and I'm goin' to do it right now.'

Before Stella realized what the killer had in mind, he had got lithely to his feet and moved towards her, reaching for her. It was done before she had any time to react. She had no chance to escape the sweep of his arm as it went around her pulling her to her feet, drawing her towards him in an irresistible grip. The man's strength was frightening. As much as she tried to struggle, it was impossible to make any impression on him. Already his face, scarred by her nails, was within inches of her own as she tried to move her head away, a scream rising to her lips.

Laredo uttered another harsh, contemptuous laugh. 'Scream if you like,' he said, 'there's no one around here to help you and — '

In spite of himself, the sight of Stella in the other's arms was too much for Frank. He stepped forward, and his foot, knocking against a pile of rocks, sent them scattering across the floor of the tunnel. Laredo whirled, releasing his grip on the girl slightly as he turned.

'Damn you!' he choked off. 'I said you were to watch the trail and not come sneakin' in here to — ' He broke off swiftly as Frank stepped into the pale light of the lamp.

Frank's subsequent actions were neither reasoned out, nor planned. He acted entirely according to the savage, angry instinct that boiled up within him. Before Laredo could fully release his hold on Stella's waist, Frank had leapt across the intervening space, the rage within him closely akin to madness. He did not see the girl clearly. She had somehow faded into a misty background figure on the edge of a blurring crimson haze that hovered in front of his eyes.

The only thing that Frank wanted now was to get his hands around Laredo's throat and choke the life out of him. He had a gun in his belt, but he made no attempt to use it. To choke, to hammer, to rip and destroy; these were all the things that mattered now. Laredo tried to fend him off, but the impact of Frank's body colliding with his knocked him backward, off balance, sending him crashing into the rocky wall. He struggled with no luck to get to his feet. Frank's boot caught him a hard blow on the shin as he went down and he uttered a thin bleating yelp of agony as his leg gave under him, pitching him sideways. Desperately, he brought up his arms and clamped them tightly around Frank's middle, seeking to haul himself up that way, his lips thinned back over his teeth as he forced air into his heaving lungs. There was no chance for him to reach the gun in its holster.

He knew now that he was fighting for his life against a man who would neither give nor ask for quarter.

Swinging his arm, Frank sent a chopping blow to the other's throat, waited until the other fell forward and brought up his knee into the man's face. He felt cartilage give and Laredo staggered back, blood spilling from his smashed mouth and dripping off his chin. His mashed lips leapt out in an ugly pout. Then came surging, desperate reaction from Laredo. He swung his fist savagely, a wild blow that would have missed its target completely had not Frank stumbled on a loose rock and fallen sideways. The blow hit him on the side of the face, spinning him round, almost dropping him in his tracks. He took two more blows to the head before he was able to pull his senses together and gather himself, giving ground fast.

There was a savage grin of triumph on Laredo's face now as he lunged forward, driving Frank back toward the metal wagon that stood on the steel rails a few feet away. Chance alone saved Frank at this point. In his eagerness to have it over and done with, Laredo became a trifle over-confident. Grinning viciously through his mashed features, he sent a couple of short jabbing blows into Frank's chest, then tried to reach for his injured arm. The shirt had become torn during the fight and, through the wide tear, the other had glimpsed the white bandage, knew his foe's weakness.

Frank felt pain jar redly along his arm and up into his left shoulder as the other gripped his wrist and tried to whirl him round, to bring the arm up hard against the joint.

Wildly, Frank twisted abruptly in the opposite direction, knowing it was the only chance he had. The agony in his arm momentarily threatened to pass beyond the limits of human endurance. Then he saw that the move had worked. Unable to help himself, feet slipping on the uneven ground, Laredo fell off balance, his head slamming back against the solid, unyielding metal of the truck at his back. There was a sickening crunch as his skull hit the steel. Frank felt him go limp, fall away from him, collapsing like a rag doll on to the ground at his feet.

Stella came running forward. Behind her were George and Clem Duprey, their guns out.

'You all right, Frank?' Stella's eyes were glowing stars, her face lined with a look of deep concern.

He moved his left arm experimentally, then nodded. 'Reckon I'll be fine once I get this wound bandaged up again,' he said hoarsely. 'Seems that it's open again.' There was the redness of fresh blood on his shirt. 'But that can wait until we get back to the Lazy T.'

'There's another man on watch outside,' Stella said quickly. 'Laredo said that — '

Frank placed his arm around her. 'No need to worry about him,' he said softly, drawing in a deep breath. 'He won't give any trouble now.'

Slowly they made their way back along the dark tunnel. Outside the sky was still clear, the stars so bright it seemed one had only to reach up and touch them.

★　★　★

It was the quiet time of the early morning when Austen Klagge rode into the courtyard of the Lazy T. With an air of confidence, he slid from the saddle and walked up to the porch, hammering on the door. Kent Michener opened the door, eyed the other with a stony anger, keeping his fury in check with an effort. He said slowly: 'I suppose you know that there were a dozen rifles on you all the way in, Klagge. That I have only to give the signal and you're a dead man.'

Klagge grinned. 'You think I'd ride out here alone if I thought there was the remotest chance of that, Michener? You know damned well there's nothin' you can do so long as I have your daughter. Try anything with me and she'll be dead before you see her again.'

With an effort, Michener forced his clenched fists to loosen by his sides. He said dully: 'What is it that you want here, Klagge?'

'You know damned well what I want. I made you a fair offer for this place, but you turned it down. Now you are livin' to regret that decision. You have no choice. I want you and your men out of here by nightfall.'

'And Stella?'

'She'll be delivered to you, safe and sound, in Fort Arthur. Provided you sign the deeds over to me and then get out of the territory.'

'And what is there to prevent me from tellin' the authorities in Fort Arthur what has happened?'

Klagge shrugged. 'That possibility had crossed my mind,' he admitted. 'But if you do that, just remember that I have men all over the territory and one of them can get to you and your daughter long before they ever bring me for trial. Always assumin' that anyone will take your word against mine. With the deeds in my possession, it won't be easy for you to prove you signed them under pressure.'

He grinned as he saw Michener's shoulders sag fractionally, knew that the other man was beat. Outside, in the courtyard, he heard a few riders come in from the hills. 'Don't forget what I said,' he muttered ominously. 'Any move against me and my men have orders to kill your daughter. I'm sure you won't be so foolish as to try that.'

Michener's hooded eyes pinched down. Klagge smiled once more and drew the papers from his pocket. 'That's better,' he said softly. 'Now just sign here and I'll be on my way.'

He held out the pen to the rancher, then stiffened abruptly as a familiar voice from the doorway at his back said: 'You won't be goin' anywhere, Klagge. This is the end of the trail for you.'

Klagge turned slowly to face Frank.

For a moment the look of confidence remained on his features. Then it faded slowly as Stella stepped into the room. His hand moved swiftly towards the shoulder holster, then stopped as he found himself staring down the barrel of Frank's gun.

'Try that and it will give me the greatest pleasure to kill you,' Frank said. 'And don't expect any help from Laredo. He's dead. But before he died, he admitted to the killin' of Fernandez. Ironic that, isn't it? Making the murderer the sheriff in Fresno City. Guess a lot of folk are goin' to change their mind about you and your friends when they hear the truth.'

Duprey stepped forward, pulled the small derringer from the shoulder holster and dropped it on to the nearby table. 'I'm takin' you back into town, Klagge,' he said tightly. 'This time you'll go to Fort Arthur for trial, and I reckon you can rely on a jury that ain't rigged.' Pausing, he said meaningly: 'I'd like a talk with you, George, before we pull out, and you too, Kent.'

When they had gone, Frank turned towards Stella. Her eyes were grey and luminous, warm and glowing, her cheeks deeply glowing with colour. She held out a slim hand. 'I think that Clem can see things a little more clearly than you,' she said in a soft murmur.

THE END

We do hope that you have enjoyed reading this large print book.

Did you know that all of our titles are available for purchase?

We publish a wide range of high quality large print books including:
Romances, Mysteries, Classics
General Fiction
Non Fiction and Westerns

Special interest titles available in large print are:
The Little Oxford Dictionary
Music Book, Song Book
Hymn Book, Service Book

Also available from us courtesy of Oxford University Press:
Young Readers' Dictionary
(large print edition)
Young Readers' Thesaurus
(large print edition)

For further information or a free brochure, please contact us at:
Ulverscroft Large Print Books Ltd.,
The Green, Bradgate Road, Anstey,
Leicester, LE7 7FU, England.
Tel: (00 44) **0116 236 4325**
Fax: (00 44) **0116 234 0205**

STONE MOUNTAIN

Concho Bradley

The stage robbery had been accomplished by an old woman. Twine Fourch had never heard of a female being a highway robber before. He followed the trail all the way to a dilapidated log cabin up Stone Mountain. What happened after that no one could believe even after townsmen from Jefferson found the old log house and the skeletal dying old woman. But before the mystery could be solved there would be two unnecessary killings, a bizarre suicide and a lynching.

GUNS OF THE GAMBLER

M. Duggan

Destitute gambler Ben Crow arrives in Mallory keen to claim his inheritance, only to discover that rancher Edward Bacon has other ideas. Set up by Miss Dorothy, who had fooled him completely, Ben finds himself dangling on the end of a rope. Saved from death, Ben sets off in pursuit of Miss Dorothy, determined upon retribution. However, his quest for vengeance turns into a rescue mission when she is kidnapped by a crazy man-burning bandit.

SIDEWINDER

John Dyson

All Flynn wants is to be Marshal of Tucson, but he is framed by the territory's richest rancher, Frank Buchanan, and thrown into Yuma prison. Five years later Flynn comes out, intent on clearing his name and burning for vengeance. Fists thud, knives flash and bullets fly as he rides both sides of the law and participates in kidnapping and double-dealing. He is once again arrested for a murder of which he is innocent. Can he escape the noose a second time?

THE BLOODING OF JETHRO

Frank Fields

When Jethro Smith's family is murdered by outlaws, vengeance is the one thing on his mind. He meets the brother of one of the murderers, who attempts to exploit Jethro's grudge in the pursuit of his own vendetta. The local preacher, formerly a sheriff, teaches Jethro how to use a gun. With his new-found skills, Jethro and his somewhat unwelcome friend pit themselves against seemingly impossible odds. Whatever the outcome lead would surely fly.

SEVEN HELLS AND A SIXGUN

Jack Greer

Jim Cayman had been warned about Daphne Rankin, his boss's wife, and her little ways. When Daphne made a play for Jim and he resisted, the result was painful and about what he had feared. But suddenly matters went beyond the expected and he found himself left to die an awful death. Only then did he realise that there was far more than a woman scorned. He vowed that if he could escape from the hell-hole he would surely solve the mystery — and settle some scores.